KU-519-033

River Boy

Winner of the Carnegie Medal

'a superbly written, well-crafted story'
School Librarian

'*River Boy* has all the hallmarks of a classic . . . You are not the same
person at the end of this book.'
Carnegie Medal judges

'an accomplished, crafted book'
Times Educational Supplement

'haunting, poetic and written with great feeling.'
Mail on Sunday

'strong on mood and atmosphere'
The Guardian

'The atmosphere is haunting . . .'
The Spectator

'Bowler's writing creates indelible visual images.'
Time Out

Tim Bowler was born and brought up in Leigh-on-Sea, Essex, the
setting of his first novel, *Midget*, and he still visits there regularly. Since
leaving university, where he obtained an honours degree in Swedish and
Scandinavian Studies, he has worked in a variety of fields including
forestry and the timber trade and as a teacher of modern languages. He
now works as a freelance writer and translator of Scandinavian languages
and lives in Devon. *River Boy* was his third novel for Oxford University
Press and won the 1998 Carnegie Medal.

River Boy

Other books by Tim Bowler

Midget
Dragon's Rock
Shadows

River Boy

Tim Bowler

Oxford University Press

Oxford   New York   Toronto

Oxford University Press, Great Clarendon Street,
Oxford OX2 6DP

Oxford New York
Athens Auckland Bangkok Bogotá Buenos Aires Calcutta
Cape Town Chennai Dar es Salaam Delhi Florence Hong Kong Istanbul
Karachi Kuala Lumpur Madrid Melbourne Mexico City Mumbai
Nairobi Paris São Paulo Singapore Taipei Tokyo Toronto Warsaw

and associated companies in
Berlin Ibadan

Oxford is a trade mark of Oxford University Press

First published 1997
Reprinted 1998 (twice)
First published in this paperback edition 1999

British Library Cataloguing in Publication Data
Data available

Cover illustration by Sam Hadley

ISBN 0 19 275035 6

Printed in Great Britain by Cox & Wyman Ltd, Reading, Berkshire

For Larry,
who knows about rivers.

'All the rivers run into the sea; yet the sea is not full:
unto the place from whence the rivers come,
thither they return again.'
(Ecclesiastes 1:7)

Chapter One

It didn't start with the river boy. It started, as so many things started, with Grandpa, and with swimming. It was only later, when she came to think things over, that she realized that in a strange way the river boy had been part of her all along, like the figment of a dream.

And the dream was her life.

Half-past nine in the morning and the pool was crowded already. That was the down-side to summer holidays, especially hot ones like this, but she knew she shouldn't grumble: she'd been here since six thirty, together with the usual hard-core of serious swimmers, and she'd managed a leisurely four miles without interruption.

But she did grumble; the mere sight of all these people flopping in like lemmings made her want to shout with frustration. She wasn't ready to stop yet, not by a long way. She had energy left and she wanted to use it.

She stuck to her lane, doggedly ploughing length after length, trying to ignore the splash of other swimmers. Sometimes she'd found that if she just forced herself to keep on swimming up and down her lane without stopping or swerving, the other users of the pool seemed by some collective telepathy to accept that space as hers, and leave it to her. But that wouldn't work today: they seemed to be jumping in by the score. Another quarter of an hour and it would be unbearable.

She locked into her stroke and drove herself on, her breath beating its practised rhythm in time with the strokes, as even as the chime of a clock. In for a gulp of

1

oxygen, her mouth twisted upwards to snap its life from the air, then face down again and the long exhalation to a slow, steady count, bubbles teasing her lips like tiny fish.

She loved this rhythm; she needed it. It kept her thoughts on track when they started to wander. Sometimes, when things were going well and she was feeling secure in herself and had something pleasant to think about, she was happy to let them wander; but if she was tiring or feeling vulnerable or worrying about Grandpa again, she focused on that rhythm and it settled her, sometimes even when she wasn't swimming.

But she was always swimming. She needed to swim. To be deprived of swimming would be like a perverse kind of drowning. She loved the sensation of power and speed, the feeling of glistening in a bed of foam, even the strange isolation of mind in this watery cocoon. Distance swimming was as much about will as about technique; and she knew she was strong in both. All she needed now, to set that will alight, was a big swimming challenge; something to test herself against. Something she could one day be proud of.

She heard Grandpa's voice calling her.

'Keep going, Jess!'

She glanced up at him as she flashed by, and smiled to herself. She knew what 'keep going' meant. Dear old Grandpa: he'd only been here twenty minutes and he was bored already. He ought to know by now that he could never fool her, of all people. His concentration span had always been short, except when he was painting, and his temper shorter still. Yet for some reason he always liked to come and watch her swimming.

She reached the far end of the pool, turned and kicked off the wall, and looked for Grandpa again. He'd wandered round to the shallow end and was standing there, watching some children. He was ready to go; but maybe she could squeeze in a couple more lengths to finish off. She plunged down towards him, feeling for some reason slightly apprehensive. The children in the shallow end blocked her lane but they broke apart as she approached and she slipped in between them, wondering whether she should stop.

Grandpa called out again.

'Everything's fine, Jess. Keep going.'

She kicked off the wall and headed back down the pool, suddenly desperately uneasy. Something was wrong but she couldn't work out what it was. His words rang in her head: everything's fine, everything's fine. And yet there was something in the very contrariness of Grandpa that told her he was trying to conceal something. He was such a stubborn, prickly old man, he would always say everything was fine.

Especially when it wasn't.

She broke out of her stroke and stopped, treading water, and searched for Grandpa. There he was, still standing by the shallow end, watching the children. He looked all right; no different from before. Just bored. Perhaps she was imagining all this. He saw her and raised a hand to wave.

Then, to her horror, clutched it over his heart and crashed into the pool.

The hospital managed to keep him three days. He was meant to have stayed much longer but, being Grandpa, as soon as he'd decided he was feeling better, he rang for a taxi and, to the consternation of doctors, nurses, and a protesting taxi driver who was convinced his cab was about to turn into a hearse, discharged himself. As he informed the exasperated consultant, the family was going on holiday on August 20th and, as this was the 19th, he needed to get home to pack.

So he was home again.

She knew it was a mistake. Much as she'd been yearning to see him back, she knew the moment he

3

arrived that this time even his independent spirit had misled him. He'd turned up at the door looking like a skeleton and they'd put him straight to bed. He seemed barely well enough to move, let alone go on holiday.

The next morning, at Grandpa's insistence, they started packing, though only after Dad had forced him to agree to let them call out Doctor Phelps. Jess liked Doctor Phelps but went up to her room when she heard him at the door. She knew what the outcome would be: once Grandpa had set his mind on something, that was that, and if he'd decided he was going on holiday, nothing anyone could say or do would change his plans. So Doctor Phelps, pleasant man though he was, would get short shrift.

She sat down at the desk and stared at the swimming medals on the shelf with her birthday cards propped up among them, the big jokey one from Grandpa most prominent of all. But neither swimming medals nor being fifteen seemed relevant right now.

She frowned and let her gaze wander out of the window into the street, already clogged with cars and buses and taxis struggling towards the city centre. The omens for a good holiday seemed remote indeed.

Some time later she heard a tap at the door.

'Come in, Mum,' she said, not looking round.

Mum came in and put a hand on her shoulder.

'Do you recognize all our knocks?'

Jess glanced up at her and tried to smile.

'Suppose so. Has Doctor Phelps gone?'

'Yes.'

'And was Grandpa horrible to him?'

'Not horrible. Just . . . you know . . . '

'Grandpa-rish.'

Mum laughed.

'Yes. Grandpa-rish.'

'So we're still going on holiday?'

'Yes.'

Jess sighed.

'He shouldn't be home. And we shouldn't be going on holiday. He's not well enough.'

'I know. But let's not think the worst. He's such a stubborn character he'll probably pull through out of sheer bloody-mindedness just to prove us all wrong.'

Jess scowled down at the desk.

'I still think he should be in hospital.'

'Well, you won't change him,' said Mum. 'You know what he's like. Dad and I aren't happy about it either. If he has another turn where we're going, it might not be easy to get him to a hospital. It's a very isolated place, apparently. But he's set on going so let's just hope it does him some good.'

'He needs rest. Lots of rest.'

'Try telling him that. Anyway, are you ready?'

'Yes.'

'Well done.' Mum leaned forward suddenly. 'Jess, give your dad plenty of support. I know you will anyway but, remember, if it's hard for you, it's worse for him. OK? See you downstairs.'

Mum kissed her and left the room, and Jess thought over what she had said. She was right, of course: it must be worse for Dad, as Grandpa's son, and an only son at that, even though the two of them seemed constantly at loggerheads. But that was hardly surprising: they were such different men, one fiercely independent, fiercely driven; the other mild and unambitious.

She glanced out of the window and saw Dad in the street, fitting the roof box to the car, and smiled to herself. That was about the extent of Dad's ambition: DIY projects that never quite came off. He'd always liked making things. Working with his hands seemed to take some of the tension out of him after a day's teaching, though whenever he produced anything, the unfortunate object never quite looked as if it had come into the world with a willing heart.

The roof box was no exception; and the fact that everyone in the street now called it 'the coffin' did nothing to make her feel more comfortable.

He walked back into the house and a moment later she heard his voice as he climbed the stairs.

'Jess? You packed?'

She picked up her suitcase, hurried forward and opened the door of her room to find him standing there.

'I'll take the case,' he said.

'It's OK.'

'No, here.' He reached out to take it, then suddenly, as though on an impulse, put his arm round her instead and held her to him. She looked up at him, expecting him to speak, but he didn't; he just held her, his eyes staring over her head; then—just as suddenly—he let her go.

'First day for ages you haven't been swimming,' he said.

'Didn't feel like it somehow.'

'I know.'

He took the suitcase and started down the stairs. She followed, trying to see the expression on his face but unable to catch it.

'How long will it take us to get there?' she said.

'Hard to say, not having been there before. There'll probably be lots of tourists on the roads. That could slow us down. And it's a very remote place. Miles from anywhere and difficult to get to, judging from the map.' He glanced at his watch. 'Can't see us getting there before dark.'

He stopped at the bottom of the stairs and left the suitcase with the others. Mum appeared at the kitchen door.

'Is the coffin on the car?' she said.

Dad frowned.

'Yes. But, listen, can we stop calling it that?'

'Pop won't mind,' she said. 'He was the one who called it that in the first place.'

6

Dad looked at her.

'It wasn't him I was thinking of.'

Mum's eyes softened at once.

'We'll call it the roof box,' she said quietly. 'Jess, can you go and check Pop's all right?'

Grandpa was in the sitting room in his favourite chair, his head thrown to one side, and she thought at first he was sleeping. Then she caught a sparkle in the eyes.

'How are you, Grandpa?' she said.

'Still dodging the undertaker. Is the coffin ready?'

She chuckled.

'Dad's just fixed it on the car. But how are you really?'

'Fine.' He glanced at her, then gave a wink. 'Long as you're around.'

She looked away, trying not to show how much it hurt her to see him as frail as this. The Grandpa she'd always known had been a man of vigour, energy, passion, despite his age. It seemed somehow unjust to see him any other way. She tried to take her mind from the thoughts she feared most.

'Do you think you'll remember the place?' she said.

''Course I will. I was born there.'

'But you were only fifteen when you left.'

'That's right. Same age as you.'

'And you've never been back since. So it'll be different.'

He sniffed.

'I'll remember it. You wouldn't forget this place, would you?'

She looked down.

What was it about Grandpa that was so reassuring yet so unsettling? He seemed utterly unconcerned about his condition. He had always been fearless, or at least appeared so, yet somewhere within himself he must have pondered the dark possible outcome of all this: the thing that preyed on her mind and no doubt on Mum's and Dad's minds too; the thing no one mentioned.

7

She saw her father at the door.

'All right, Dad?' he said. 'Jess looking after you?'

She wished he wouldn't keep raising his voice every time he spoke to Grandpa. He'd only started doing it since yesterday and it made it seem as though the heart attack had not only weakened Grandpa but rendered him deaf as well. Sooner or later there was bound to be a caustic response. But Grandpa merely raised an eyebrow this time.

'Jess is looking after me fine.'

'Well, let's get you in the car, then.'

He let them help him to his feet, then quickly waved them aside and reached for his stick. Jess stood back and watched his painful progress out of the sitting room, Dad hovering anxiously close by in case he fell. Mum was waiting in the hall.

'All right, Pop?'

'Yes, yes, for God's sake. How can I be anything else with you lot fussing over me all the time?'

Mum chuckled and stood aside to let them pass; then she caught Jess by the arm.

'Come with me,' she said.

Jess followed her through to the study and there on the table, propped against the wall, was an unframed painting, unmistakably one of Grandpa's yet unlike anything he had done before; and clearly nowhere near finished.

'Do you know anything about this?' said Mum.

Jess shook her head.

'I've never seen it before. I didn't know he was working on anything.'

Mum looked hard at her.

'He did this last night.'

'You mean—?'

'When he got back from the hospital. We put him to bed—remember?—and he must have waited till we'd all turned in, then got out again and come downstairs and fetched his brushes and what have you, and worked

8

through the night. And now he tells me he wants to take the thing on holiday to finish it. I don't know what drives that man, I really don't.'

Jess stared at the picture.

It was so different from his usual work. There was a river, which dominated the scene, not a river she recognized and perhaps not even a real one at all, just a fantasy river. The picture was strange and amorphous, so different from his other paintings, yet it was eerily beautiful. The banks were a subtle hint of green that the eye barely took in, being somehow drawn into the pale waters and away towards a hidden sea. There were no animals, no birds, no people; and it felt right that way. There seemed no place for living things in this remote vision. Yet for some reason she found herself thinking of the coming of autumn, after a long, rich summer.

Mum spoke again.

'It's got a name.'

There was something in her voice—something too casual, too detached—that betrayed her excitement. And Jess knew why. Grandpa never gave his pictures names. He just painted them and left others to make sense of them, if they could. Mum turned the picture over and pointed to the words Grandpa had scrawled there. Jess read them aloud.

'River Boy.'

The words seemed to carry a strange resonance, as though they were somehow important to her, yet why that should be so she could not tell. And there was a further mystery.

She looked round at Mum.

'There's no boy.'

'Exactly. Strange, isn't it—I mean, for him to be so specific. Still, he hasn't finished it yet so maybe he's going to put the boy in later. I made the mistake of asking him about it.'

'Mum! You should have known better.'

9

'I know, but I couldn't resist it. It's such an unusual picture, especially having a name. I suppose you can guess the response.'

Jess didn't need to guess. She knew what Grandpa's response would have been.

'He told you it's not up to the artist to explain a painting because each picture has its own life and its own language, just like a poem, and we either understand it or we don't. And he said painting's hard enough work as it is without having to waste time telling every idiot—'

'Ignoramus, he said.'

'Every ignoramus what the thing means. And if artists had to explain their pictures to every Tom, Dick, and Harry who came along, they'd never get any work done. And he said—'

Mum interrupted her, laughing.

'Something like that. Anyway, I was hoping you might know something about this painting, seeing as you seem to be a sort of a muse for him.'

'Muse?'

'Someone who inspires an artist.'

She knew what the word meant. Grandpa had often used it when she went to watch him paint, but generally it was just to say that the muse wasn't being kind to him today, or that he'd have to be nice to the muse today as he had a difficult bit to work on, or something like that. He'd never suggested the muse had anything to do with her. Indeed, she'd always thought he meant some kind of goddess, not a human being at all. And it was hard to imagine anyone, even a goddess, having any influence over someone as wilful as Grandpa.

'He doesn't need me to inspire him,' she said. 'He's been painting all his life.'

Mum ran her finger round the edge of the painting, as though debating whether to answer; then she spoke, in a quiet, thoughtful voice.

'But he's only really found himself in his painting

10

since you were born. His earlier pictures all lacked something. They had plenty of technical skill, but the magic wasn't there.' She paused. 'But after you were born, it's like something started to motivate him, and it's gone on motivating him ever since.'

'But he's never called me a muse or anything like that.'

'He wouldn't. And he's never said anything to Dad or me either. He probably doesn't even see it that way himself and if anyone asked him about it, he'd say they're talking rubbish. But there's something—I don't know what it is—but something he gets from you, something really important to him. Dad and I both feel it.' She stroked Jess on the cheek. 'I don't know why I'm telling you this, but keep it to yourself and don't let it make you vain—not that you would. Just treat it as a sign of his love.'

Jess looked back at the painting and said nothing.

'So you don't know anything about the river boy?' said Mum.

'Sorry.'

'Not to worry. Well, let's get going. Bring the picture out to the car, can you? Not that I can see him having the energy to finish it on holiday, whatever he thinks. You know how worked up he gets when he's painting.'

Jess picked it up.

'I'll be along in a moment.'

'Well, don't hang around. We've got a hell of a journey in front of us.'

'OK.'

She waited until Mum had gone, then stared down at the picture again; and the words slid into her mind once more.

River Boy.

It was strange, but no doubt, as Mum said, Grandpa would put the boy in later. If he was strong enough to paint. That was the big worry. He might never lift a brush again, though she doubted that. He was so obsessive about a painting once he had started it, and this one—this one she sensed was important to him. And, for some reason, also to her.

She didn't know why. She only knew that the more she looked at it, the more the presence of the absent boy seemed to grow, until finally it overwhelmed everything, the banks and the sky and even the river itself, pulling her into the picture and onwards, irresistibly, towards the sea.

Chapter Two

The journey took longer than even Dad had anticipated. Conversation died away and came back, and died away and came back, and finally died away altogether. Jess dozed through much of the trip. And into her mind came sleepy images of Grandpa.

She saw pictures of him playing with her in the garden when she was very small, letting her climb all over him, pretending she was too strong for him; pictures of him taking her to hospital the time she fell from the swing and hurt her leg; pictures of him teaching her to ride a bike, holding on to the saddle to steady her and calling out encouragement when he realized she was afraid. And most of all, pictures of him painting; and pictures of him watching her while she swam.

She opened her eyes and saw another picture, the picture of an old man slumped on the back seat beside her, fast asleep, his chin on his chest, his head tipped slightly towards her. He seemed so fragile, especially with his eyes closed so that she couldn't see the fire that usually blazed there. She glanced at Mum in the front seat and saw her nodding, too, then caught Dad's eye in the car mirror.

'All right, Jess?' he said.

'Yes.' It wasn't true and she suspected he sensed it but he didn't press her. She stared out of the window at the dipping sun. 'How much longer?'

'Few hours yet. Tired?'

'Yes.'

'We'll have a good rest when we get there.'

'Do you think there'll be anybody there who remembers Grandpa?'

'Doubt it. Depends on whether anyone from his boyhood days has stayed on in the area, and whether they're still alive.' He glanced round as though to check Grandpa was still asleep. 'He hasn't kept in touch with anyone, that's for sure. You know what he's like for blocking out the past. He says he's got a name to look up. Someone called Alfred who used to live round there. But I think it's very unlikely anybody'll know him. And even if they do, we probably won't meet them. It's a very remote place. The nearest house to us is about two miles, apparently. Ah, well. It's what he wanted.'

She gazed out at the fields and hills, so different from the urban landscape she'd grown up with, and wondered about the point of all this. They'd planned the trip before Grandpa's heart attack, and it had been his own wish: he wanted to go back and see his boyhood home again, something he had never expressed the slightest desire to do.

That in itself was out of character: he'd always scorned looking back, as though it were a weakness. But memories, she knew, must be painful for him. Having lost both parents at the age of fifteen in the fire that destroyed their house, he had every right to think hard of the past.

Yet now they were going back.

She looked at him close beside her, hunched and weak, still fast asleep. Maybe he would surprise her; maybe on this holiday he would regain his health, become strong again. But the more she looked at him, the more her fears grew.

Amidst those fears, her eyes closed once more.

She woke to the sound of running water. And Dad's voice, weary but relieved.

14

'Wake up, everybody. We're here.'

She blinked and looked about her. Night had fallen but through the window she could see the dark outline of trees. Dad opened the driver's door to climb out and the interior light flashed onto the sluggish confusion of their faces. Mum twisted round in her seat.

'Everybody OK? Pop?'

'Yes,' mumbled Grandpa, clearly not so.

'Jess?'

'I'm OK.'

Mum yawned.

'Thought we'd never get here. That road from Braymouth seemed to wind on for ever.'

Jess pushed her door open and stepped out, and the sound of the water rushed over her with greater force. She looked to the right and there, glistening under the moon, was the stream.

Mum climbed out of the car, walked over and put an arm round her.

'Beautiful place. Hope it's not too cut off for you.'

Jess said nothing: she was still captivated by the sound of the stream. Dad's voice broke into her reverie.

'Let's take a look at the cottage.'

She turned round and gave a start: she'd been so fascinated by the river that she hadn't even noticed the dusky shape of the cottage close by. It stood to the left of her with tall trees behind and the river twisted past it only a short distance away.

'Dad?' she said. 'Did you say there aren't any other houses?'

'Afraid not. We're more or less on our own here. There's a house about two miles away along the Braymouth road. That's where Mr and Mrs Gray live. They're the owners of this place. They've got several holiday cottages, Mr Gray told me, but they're mostly round Braymouth. That's the only community round here and it's only an average-size town. There's not much else, just the odd farm or smallholding.'

She looked about her, still absorbed by the sound of the stream. She was glad they were on their own here; she didn't want any other communities. Just the four of them, and this place; that was enough. Braymouth could be as far away as it liked.

'How far's Braymouth?' she said.

'About twenty-five miles as the crow flies,' said Dad. 'At least forty by road once you've twisted about and climbed over the hills, and probably about the same if you were to follow the base of the valley. I expect this little stream ends up at Braymouth.'

'It does,' said Grandpa in a breathless voice behind them.

They turned and saw him struggling to lift himself out of the car. Dad hurried round to help him.

'Sorry, Dad,' he said. 'Here, let me . . . '

With an effort and much assistance Grandpa stood up and gazed about him in the darkness. Jess watched him, wondering what he was thinking, being here again after all these years. He sniffed the air suddenly and looked round at Dad.

'And it's not just a little stream,' he said grumpily. 'It turns into a good-sized river just down from here.' He glanced at the cottage. 'So this is where we're staying.'

'Yes.' Dad hesitated. 'And I don't want any complaints. You've no idea how much trouble I had finding accommodation in this place.'

'Who did you say owns it?'

'People called Gray.'

'Never heard of them.'

'You won't have. Anyway, let's get inside.'

'I'll walk with Pop,' said Mum.

'Don't bother me,' said Grandpa. 'I'm all right.'

Dad switched on a torch and led the way towards the cottage.

'Mr Gray said he'd leave the key on the ledge over the door.'

'Very trusting,' said Grandpa.

'Well, when I told him how late we'd be rolling up, I don't think he fancied staying up. I expect we'll see him in the morning.'

'There's the ledge,' said Mum. She felt over it. 'And here's the key.'

She unlocked the door and they entered. Jess found a light switch and flicked it on to reveal a narrow hall stretching ahead of them with stairs at the end.

It seemed clean and comfortable enough downstairs. There was a decent-sized sitting room, a small loo with a basin, and a large games room with a table tennis table dominating one half of it and a cupboard stuffed full of balls, bats, and rackets of various types. In the corner, as they'd requested, was a put-up bed ready assembled.

Mum walked over and examined it.

'It's quite springy, Pop. Will you be all right on this?'

'I've slept on worse.'

'I'm sorry. Putting you in here was the only solution we could think of.'

'I expect I'll cope.'

They wandered through to inspect the kitchen and Grandpa slumped straight into a chair. He said nothing but Jess could tell from his face that he was desperately tired, desperately anxious to be left alone. She saw a note on the table and handed it to Dad who quickly read it through.

'It's from Mr Gray,' he said. 'He says the only place to get food is Braymouth but he's put milk and butter in the fridge and bread, tea, and sugar in the pantry. That's nice of him. Where's the pantry?'

'Here,' said Jess, opening a door.

'He told us on the phone there's a freezer,' said Mum, looking about her.

'Over there,' said Dad.

She looked it over.

'Bigger than I expected. That's good. And not a bad-sized fridge. Still, I suppose you have to stock up well out here.'

Jess caught Dad's eye and they both smiled. Mum always packed enough provisions for a round-the-world trip, no matter where they were going. They probably wouldn't need to go to Braymouth at all if they didn't want to.

They left Grandpa sitting in the kitchen and checked the upstairs rooms. There was a bathroom and two bedrooms, a double and a small single. Jess walked into hers and looked around. It had a table, an armchair, a built-in wardrobe, and a comfortable enough bed; it seemed fairly welcoming. She wandered over to the window and saw the stream running past barely thirty feet away.

Mum spoke from behind her in the doorway.

'I'm a bit bothered about the noise of that stream. We didn't realize there was a river running so close.'

'I don't mind it.'

'You haven't tried sleeping here yet. I hope it doesn't keep you awake. Our room's noisy enough and that's on the other side of the house.'

'I'll be fine, Mum. Honestly.'

She saw anxiety on Mum's face and tried to think of something to reassure her.

'I like the sound of the river,' she said eventually. 'I really do. It makes me think of swimming. I'd have chosen this room even if there'd been others free. Anyway, all that matters is that Grandpa's comfortable downstairs.'

Mum walked over to the window and gazed down at the stream, frowning.

'I just hope he is,' she said.

Jess soon found Mum was right. The stream did keep her awake. Yet it was strange: something about the sound seemed to rest her, almost as much as sleep itself.

She lay back in the bed, watching the play of moonlight upon the window and listening to the water below, racing on towards the sea. It was impossible to ignore the music of the stream—it so dominated everything—but she soon found she didn't want to ignore it. She liked it; and the more she listened, the more it seemed like conversation.

Strange conversation, and constant, too, as though the river had much to impart. Perhaps Grandpa was listening as well. Perhaps he was lying awake right now, just as she was, drinking in this falling chatter. Perhaps, being born here, he understood it better than she did. He must have listened to the river many a time.

She sat up, frowning.

Thoughts of Grandpa always filled her with a mixture of feelings: admiration at his strength; tenderness at his vulnerability. It was hard to think of Grandpa dying. She had always imagined he would go on for years—and perhaps he would. Perhaps he would astonish them all. He was old, but not that old.

She listened to the river again and finally its restlessness mastered her, matching perhaps the restlessness she felt within herself, and she stood up, put her dressing-gown on and wandered to the window and leaned down, elbows on the sill, her chin cupped in her hands, and watched the stream as it ran past, talking to the night.

'What are you saying?' she murmured to it. 'What are you trying to tell me?'

The waters slipped past, dark and sleek, gurgling over the rocks just down from her window, then twisting away towards the lower ground hidden beyond the house. And part of her seemed to run with them, all the way to the sea.

She sighed.

There was something strange about this place, unsettling even, yet not scary. It was as though there were a spirit here, not some ghoul or creeping shade, but a spirit of the river, of the trees and hills, a spirit running through all this like a magic charm.

The waters ran on, tinkling like a musical box.

She shivered slightly and pulled her dressing-gown more tightly around her, then, on an impulse, walked to the door of her room, opened it, and listened, trying to block out the sound of the river and hear the steady breathing of her parents.

There it was, Dad's anyway, and that was enough. Mum famously slept through everything, but Dad was the one who generally had trouble dropping off, though once he was asleep, he usually stayed asleep, and everyone could hear it.

She tiptoed down the stairs, feeling her way carefully, unsure where the light switch was in case she needed it. At the bottom she stopped, then, as softly as she could, entered the sitting room. There was the dark shape of the coffin, waiting to be fully unpacked in the morning, and, at the far end, the door to Grandpa's makeshift bedroom. She crept forward, put her ear close to it and listened, trying to hear the sound of breathing.

There was none.

She felt a flutter of panic and pushed the door open. He was lying in the bed, his face thrown back, his mouth wide open as if in a scream. She started forward, knocking the edge of the table tennis table as she did so—then he spoke.

'It's all right. I'm OK.'

He sounded tired but she was relieved to hear his voice. She felt her breath slow down again.

'Come and sit here,' he said.

She walked over and sat on the edge of the bed, close to him.

'Take my hand,' he said, struggling to free his arm from beneath the sheet.

She helped him and took his hand. It seemed so withered now, not like it used to be. Again she thought back to the days when she had been little and his hands had held her and made her feel safe. Now those hands were taking strength from hers.

'Can't you sleep?' he said.

She shook her head.

'Neither can I,' he said. 'I keep thinking how different this place feels to what I remember.' He looked at her hard, his eyes almost steely against the darkness. 'Everything changes, Jess. Everything. Nothing stays the same. Nothing lasts for ever. There's no use fighting it. We have to accept it.'

She knew what he was telling her and she didn't want to hear it. She didn't want to think of change. She wanted to think of everything being the same for ever. And even if some things did have to change, she didn't want them to change now. Some other time, perhaps, when she was good and ready and able to accept them.

He chuckled suddenly.

'Tell you one thing that won't have changed. Chap called Alfred, if he's still alive. He used to live round here when I was a boy. Same age as me. His folks had a cottage about two miles from here. Might even be the one those people—what are they called? Gray—are now living in. Can't imagine Alfred'd be any different. He was one of those characters you could never imagine doing anything unusual. He's probably living round here somewhere if he's still . . . if he's still . . . alive . . . '

His voice was dying away, and the slight pressure of his hand loosening in hers. She let it rest on top of the sheet and waited for a few moments.

Grandpa was asleep.

She stood up and walked to the door, and closed it quietly behind her, then made her way through the sitting room towards the hall. And, as she did so, she caught in the window the glow of moonlight on water. And the sound of the river came back, rushing upon her like a cascade of spells.

Chapter Three

She woke to that sound and to a frolic of birdsong. The air was cool and she felt snatches of breeze through the open window. She rubbed her eyes and glanced towards it, and saw tree-tops moving against a pale sky.

It felt early but she had no notion of what time it was. She reached down to the floor and felt for the watch she had sleepily dropped there the night before.

Five thirty.

It didn't seem possible that she'd slept so little yet felt so rested. The river was calling her already and she jumped out of bed, put on her swimsuit and crept from the room.

No sound from Mum and Dad except for Dad's steady breathing as before. They would probably sleep for some time yet, Dad especially after all his driving, though perhaps anxiety about Grandpa or just the atmosphere of this unknown place would wake them earlier than they might like. She tiptoed down to Grandpa's room and glanced round the door.

His head was back, his mouth open, and his breathing, unlike Dad's, was short and fitful; but he was at least asleep. She hurried back to the hall and out through the front door.

The sound of the birds broke upon her again, and with it, as always, the ripple of the stream. She gazed about her, wonderstruck at the beauty that daylight had revealed.

The cottage, she now saw, was at the base of a great hill which stretched up to the left of her, the river coursing down it through dense woodland. The trees were especially thick close to the cottage, but further up she saw patches of clear ground with craggy outcrops.

The cottage itself, though bordered by trees, occupied a small clearing fed from the right by the little lane which had brought them from Braymouth. There the car sat, moist with dew and looking curiously out of place. But what caught her eye most was the view beyond.

It was a valley, cleaved through by the snaking river, with high slopes on either side and, again, dense patches of woodland interspersed with rocky clearings. She walked to the edge of the water and knelt down.

It was so beautiful, this stream, only about fifteen feet across at this point, yet it moved with restless speed, drawing its power from the steepness of the slope. She stepped into the water and the chill made her draw breath, but the sharpness was invigorating; she seemed to feel the vitality of the whole river as it raced past her legs.

She walked downstream, staying in the water. The river was shallow here, barely up to her knees, and the bed, though stony and uneven, was easy underfoot and not too slippery. She left the cottage behind her and waded down towards the base of the valley.

The ground continued to fall but only a short way further. With almost dramatic suddenness it merged with the valley floor and flattened out, and she saw, through a canopy of trees, the river widen before her and wend its path onwards.

The change was almost startling. What had been a rushing whippet of a creature had, in what seemed the twinkling of an eye, become a long, almost languid beast, no longer hurrying but dawdling on its way. She waded down to where the tree-cover ended and the valley floor checked the plashing descent of the stream.

The current was still strong here, where the water broke its fall, but it quickly seemed to slacken, and further down the river, at the first point of its meander, there seemed no energy left at all, though she knew that was an illusion. It must be moving quite fast, even out there. But there was only one way to test the strength of a river.

She took another step forward. The ground fell with unexpected sharpness and the water level seemed to jump from her knees to her waist. She stopped for a moment and scanned the river before her.

It wasn't that she doubted her own ability; when it came to swimming, she trusted her own skill and strength more than almost anyone she knew. But this was an unknown river. There could be reeds, or other dangers she didn't know about. As a townee, she'd had little experience of the countryside, and none at all of swimming in rivers.

But the temptation was too great, and it looked safe enough. She took a deep breath and pushed herself into the water. It still felt cool, though not as bracing as when she had first stepped into it, and she liked the clean, luxuriant feeling as she swept down with the current.

She swam breast-stroke and kept her head above the surface, not ready to go right under until she had settled herself and felt safe, and trusted the water. After a few strokes she stopped swimming, and stretched out a foot for the bottom.

There it was, nice and firm and somewhat pebbly, but the water had deepened more quickly than she'd expected, and was already up to her chest. She looked back at the trees she had left behind her.

The current had pushed her quickly down, with very little effort on her part. Instinctively she started to swim back against it. Now she felt the true force of the river, and it was strong, though not, to her relief, too much for her. Breast-stroke kept her level with the bank, and with an effort she found she could make a little headway against it; but crawl would be no problem. She put her feet on the bottom again and peered down through the water.

It was clear and she could see the bed easily, and her feet moving about as she kept her balance against the current. She relaxed at last: this water was friendly enough. There was nothing to fear here. She could dive now.

She didn't go deep, just enough to douse her head and come straight up, and then she was swimming again, against the current and with a comfortable crawl, her favourite stroke; and the current was not her master.

She swam as far as the trees, then turned and glided back once more, letting the energy of the river take her. She didn't need to test herself now. She could conquer the river, at least at this point, and if the current grew too strong further down, she could always climb onto the bank and walk back.

But she quickly realized this might prove difficult. Parts of the bank were clear but other stretches were lined with thorn and dense vegetation. There was no discernible path as far as she could tell.

Moreover, the meander of the river itself appeared to impede straight walking. The only way to follow the river, apart from being in or on the water itself, seemed to be along the valley peaks, and the climb to them did not look an easy one. She swam to the side of the river and clung to a clump of reed.

She was a good hundred yards downstream now and the current had done most of the work. She glanced down and saw the bottom of the river curving beneath her about seven feet below. It seemed strange to find deep water so close to the bank but this was not the pool back home, or the sea: this was something new, something exciting; something she had to learn about. She pushed off and swam towards a small clearing on the other side.

The current grew noticeably weaker as she crossed and she saw the river bed rise towards the other side.

She stopped by the far bank and found that she could stand; and the water came only to her waist.

She looked about her. It was so fascinating, this river, so full of secrets. Certainly her first impression had been wrong. The current looked slow here, and on this side of the river it was, but there was a deceptive force, especially where the water was deeper. She started to swim back.

Again, to her relief, the current was unable to resist her, but she felt its will against hers and knew, as stroke followed stroke, that to swim against it for any length of time would be impossible. In the end, the river would win. Fortunately this time she only had a hundred yards to go. Yet she found, as she drove herself upstream, that even with the crawl she had to work hard; and she was curiously relieved to reach the canopy of trees from where she had started.

It was time to go back. Mum and Dad might be up, and maybe worrying about her, though they'd probably have come down to the river by now, knowing where she'd be. She waded over to the bank where there was a clearing which stretched up to the lane and on to the cottage, and started to climb out.

Then stopped, her body tensed.

Someone was near; someone was watching her. She could feel it.

She whirled round, her eyes darting over the river, the banks, the lane.

But there was no one in sight.

She relaxed, hauled herself onto the bank, and started to walk back towards the cottage. But even as she chided herself for being fanciful, the feeling started to grow that she had not been—and was not—alone.

Chapter Four

'I'm not sitting in that thing,' said Grandpa, scowling.

He hobbled on his stick over to the stream and stood there, his back firmly towards them.

Jess looked at Dad, standing with her in front of the cottage, his hand on the wheelchair he had brought from home. He looked tense and unsure of himself, as he so often was with his father. She wished Grandpa wouldn't be so hard on him all the time.

She glanced up at the sky. The sun was already some way above the peaks and the valley was warming up fast, though it was only half-past ten; and, judging from the lack of cloud, they were in for a scorcher.

She thought of the strange feeling she had had down in the river, of someone being near; and looked about her again.

But still she saw no one.

Her father cleared his throat.

'Come on, Dad. The wheelchair'll make life easier for all of us.'

Grandpa didn't look round but grumbled an answer, just audible above the sound of the stream.

'I'm not being pushed about like a supermarket trolley when I can still walk.'

Mum put her head out of the window to the kitchen where she'd been doing the washing up.

'But, Pop, we wanted to take you round a bit. See where your old house was.'

'There's nothing to see. It burnt down, for God's sake. Who wants to look at an empty space?'

'Don't you even want to visit the place where it was?'

'No.'

'But what about finding your old friend?'

'He'll be pushing up daisies by now. Or he should be. And if he's not, then another day won't make any difference. I didn't come here to see him. I came here to paint. You can go off if you want to. I'm getting on with my picture.'

Jess frowned at the mention of the painting. She had thought about it a great deal since Mum showed it to her yesterday, though she hadn't seen it since they packed it for Grandpa. And the image that haunted her most was that of the boy, the river boy; the boy who wasn't there.

Yes, he had to finish the picture, and soon. The tetchiness would only get worse and, besides, he needed to paint. It was like oxygen to him. Even he'd once admitted—in a rare, unguarded moment—that it was only painting that kept him on the respectable side of sanity.

She didn't know whether that was true. What she did know was that whenever he couldn't get to his work, she felt the depression of his spirit. It was like a wound in him, a wound she could almost touch, but not heal. His art—that was different: she could love that, admire that. But the pain of it . . .

She wished there didn't have to be pain. She tried to tell herself, whenever this upset her, that in some way painting for him must be like swimming was for her: just as she constantly needed water around her to feel truly herself, so he needed a brush with which to shape the visions of his inner life.

Through all the years she had known him, he had painted almost—it seemed—without pause, uninterested in the fame his gift had brought him and so hopeless with money he seemed constantly without it. The day he lost the hunger to work would truly be the end.

So no matter how difficult he was being, it was probably a good thing that he still wanted to paint.

'I can stay with Grandpa,' she said to Dad. 'You and Mum can go off.'

Mum came out and joined them.

'I do feel like a walk and we've got to go and see Mr and Mrs Gray. But one of us ought to stay behind.'

Grandpa turned round at last and leaned there, swaying on his stick, his eyes daring them to offer sympathy.

'Jess can stay with me if she wants to and you two can go walking.'

'But will you be all right?' said Dad.

'I'm not planning on snuffing it for a few hours yet.'

'You'd better not,' said Mum. 'I don't want you spoiling the holiday.'

Dad glanced at her with slight disapproval but Grandpa only laughed.

'OK,' she said. 'We'll go and see Mr and Mrs Gray and Jess can stay here.'

'You sure, Jess?' said Dad. 'I can stay behind if you want to explore with Mum.'

Mum touched him on the arm.

'She'll be fine.'

Jess caught her eye and smiled.

'We'll see you later,' said Mum and, before Dad could speak, she linked arms with him and steered him away, past the redundant wheelchair and across the clearing. Jess watched them disappear down the lane to Braymouth, then walked over to Grandpa.

He was staring up at the sky and seemed lost in thought; but he stirred suddenly and fixed his eyes upon her.

'Could you—?' he started.

But she put a finger on his lips.

'You know I will,' she said.

She'd fetched his things for him ever since she was small. It was one of those rituals she treasured, collecting his canvases and paints and palette, the rickety little easel he insisted he couldn't paint without even though he always swore at it and said he'd get a decent one some day, the even more rickety chair that everyone was sure would collapse under him any moment but which, like the easel, he had to have, and the brushes and cloths and turps and palette knife, and tea and biscuits, and anything else he asked for—and there was usually a lot—until he was finally ready for work; after which he would brook no distraction, even from her.

She had often thought how strange it was that she liked to do these things for him, especially when he could be such a tyrant. He had never asked her to help him in the beginning; but once he found out that it mattered to her, he always asked her. And now, especially now, she was glad of it.

'Where do you want to sit, Grandpa?' she said.

'By the river.'

She started to take the chair over to the stream but he called after her.

'Not there. Further down where it flattens out. Where you went swimming this morning.'

She looked round at him, startled.

'How did you—?'

'I didn't see you. I was asleep.'

'So how come you know—?'

He chuckled.

'I know you. Don't need to know any more. Suppose you haven't told your mum and dad you've been swimming in the river.'

'They've probably guessed anyway. Seeing as you have.'

'So you haven't told them.'

'I was going to. I just haven't had time.'

There was no fooling Grandpa but he didn't chide her. He turned and gazed downstream, his eyes distant.

'You'll be safe enough here. It's a friendly river, not like some. The current's not too strong, as you probably found, but it's enough to keep the reeds flat. You'll

30

come to no harm in the water, provided you show it respect.'

He glanced round the other way and nodded uphill.

'And the source is up the top there. You can't see it from here—we're too low down. If I was a bit younger, I'd take you up there myself and show you.'

She looked at the stream, more captivated than ever by it, and once again remembered the strange feelings she had had of someone being near; and though the feelings were gone now, the remembrance of them filled her with a slight unease.

She forced her attention back to the painting.

'Where shall I put the chair?'

'I'll show you.' He pushed himself off with his stick and lurched down the way Mum and Dad had gone. She hurried to help him but he waved her back.

'No, just bring the chair. I'll need something to collapse into when we get there.'

His mouth was tight, his eyes fixed on where he wanted to go. She walked beside him but said nothing, not wanting to tire him with talking. He trudged on, pressing the stick hard against the ground as he put his weight upon it.

She watched, secretly, anxious lest he fall. He looked frighteningly unsteady but as usual never seemed to think he couldn't do anything or go anywhere he wanted. They reached the clearing by the water's edge where she had climbed out of the river earlier, and he stopped.

'This is the place.'

She looked at him.

'Do you remember it?'

He stared out over the river.

'I've been dreaming about this place.' His voice sounded strangely wistful and for a moment she almost dared to think he was about to indulge in what for him was the unheard-of practice of reminiscing. But she was quickly disabused of the idea.

'Come on, then! Get a move on! Put the chair up before I conk out completely!'

She set it up by the bank, just where he wanted it, then ran back to the cottage to fetch his things. She asked no questions about the river boy as she handed him the picture.

Ten minutes later, he was at work.

He didn't talk in the beginning. He rarely talked for the first hour or so when he was working on a picture. It was as though he needed to focus his mind entirely on finding out what he wanted to say. Later, when he had found his way, he often liked to talk and sometimes even asked her what she thought of the painting he was doing.

She always wondered what, if anything, she gave him with her opinions. He usually hated being questioned about his work, and could be blunt and downright rude even to well-meaning people who showed interest. To Dad and even to Mum he could be scornful, as though they understood nothing about art, which was certainly not true.

She lay back and looked up at the sky, and pondered the enigma of Grandpa. It made no sense, his asking her opinion. She knew nothing about art. She only knew that for some reason he felt more comfortable working when she was around. Maybe Mum was right; maybe he did see her as a kind of muse, though that was hardly a word she would ever have applied to herself.

She glanced at him from time to time, taking care to make sure he didn't feel she was trying to see what he was doing. She had learnt over the years how touchy he was about people watching him when he was trying to concentrate, or, worse still, glancing over his shoulder before he was ready to show his work. But he was absorbed and had started quickly, which was a good sign. She said nothing and gazed back at the sky.

Two hours passed, and still he seemed intent and focused. He was working fast, feverishly fast, as though he wanted to wrench the picture out of himself in one convulsive effort.

Suddenly, to her dismay, he threw down the brush.

'It's no good. I can't get it right.'

She sat up and saw him scowling at the painting.

'Am I putting you off, Grandpa?'

'No, no, it's not you. It's me. Look at the damn thing.'

'Are you sure you want me to?'

' 'Course I do.' He glared at her but she knew his venom was directed not at her but at the picture; and himself. She stood up, walked round behind him, and looked over his shoulder; and gave a start.

It was still the river scene but he had added so much more. The hints of green that had suggested the river banks were darker and had touches of brown; the pale waters had flecks of silver and gold and blue; but the picture was now dominated by swirls of mist and a strange tension in the water as it was drawn down a widening mouth towards the sea. There was still a remoteness about the scene, yet it seemed more haunting, more disturbing than ever.

And still there was no boy.

'Where is it, Grandpa?'

His eyes flashed at her and she thought for a moment he was resentful at her question, and she cursed herself for asking it. She knew that, to him, after working with intensity on a painting, the vision he was trying to express was so obvious to him it did not occur to him that others could not see it as easily as he did, so their questions seemed like an insult. But she was wrong this time: he was still only angry with himself.

'It's supposed to be this river,' he said.

'But not this part.'

'No,' he said cryptically. 'Not this part.'

'I like it. I really do.' She smiled at him, glad that she didn't have to lie to him. But he only scowled more deeply.

33

'It's rubbish.'

He leant back in the chair and she wondered what she should do. He was spent now and bitterly frustrated with himself, and she foresaw troublesome hours ahead for everyone. He was difficult enough after finishing a painting, but not finishing a painting was even worse and usually meant an agony of moodiness and petulance until he was finally able to give form to the images which chafed inside him.

'Don't give up on the picture, Grandpa,' she said.

But he didn't answer. His face had darkened; his body was shuddering. Suddenly he clapped a hand to his chest.

She started forward.

'Grandpa, no!'

Chapter Five

He was losing consciousness fast. She held him upright in the chair, calling to him.

'Grandpa, please don't die.'

His eyes flickered at her but she didn't know whether he saw her.

'I'll run and find Mum and Dad,' she said.

'Don't . . . don't . . . ' he muttered. 'Don't . . . leave me . . . '

His face was screwed up in pain. She knelt beside him, thinking of Mum and Dad, and the first aid lessons she should have taken, and where the nearest telephone was, and . . .

His eyes opened wider and consciousness seemed to return, though with a struggle. He took a deep breath, and she heard how much it hurt him.

'Wheelchair,' he gasped. 'Wheelchair.'

'But—'

'Wheelchair.' His eyes focused upon her. 'Get me . . . back to the cottage. I'll . . . I'll be all right if I can . . . get to my bed.'

He grimaced and clutched at his chest again.

'I'm getting Mum and Dad,' she said.

'No!' He seized her hand and gripped it with all his strength. 'Listen, I'll be all right in a minute. It's just a turn. It'll pass. I . . . I just need to get back to my bed and rest and . . . and have my pills.' He gritted his teeth. 'The wheelchair . . . can you get it?'

She didn't want to leave him now. He was breathing more jerkily than ever and his face looked almost white, but his eyes were wide open again and at least he didn't look as though he were about to lose consciousness. And it was just possible Mum and Dad might be back at the cottage.

She stood up.

'I'll get it, Grandpa.'

She ran back to the cottage and quickly looked for Mum and Dad, but there was no sign of them. The wheelchair sat where they had left it only a short while ago. She seized the handles and raced with it back to Grandpa.

His body had sagged and his head had fallen forward on his chest, but at the sound of her footsteps he looked up. His breathing had calmed but he was still hideously pale.

'I'll help you into it,' she said.

He started to protest but she leant forward and slid her arms round his back.

'Be careful how you lift me,' he panted. 'Don't strain yourself. If you can't do it, leave me here. I'll manage. I'll—'

'Grandpa, shut up, will you?'

Somehow she pulled him towards her, helped, she knew, by the efforts he was making himself. But he was heavy; though not a bulky man, his body was wiry and tough and even in old age retained a residue of the great strength he must have had in his youth. She felt her cheek against his as she edged him, bit by bit, into the wheelchair.

He slumped back in it, struggling again for breath, and for a moment she feared another attack was coming. Then he winked at her.

'Thank you, nurse.' He turned his head away and gazed towards the river. 'I'm all right now. Just get me back to my bed.'

She frowned. He wasn't all right; he was seriously unwell and needed to be in hospital or at the very least have a doctor look at him. If only they had a telephone at the cottage so she could ring Mum and Dad on the mobile.

'Come on, Grandpa. Let's get you to your bed.'

She started to push him back up the slope. He said nothing but at least didn't seem to be getting any worse. They reached the cottage and she steered him through to his bedroom.

He looked round at her.

'I can manage now.'

'No, you can't.'

'Yes, I can.'

She didn't bother to argue but simply leaned forward and put her arms round him again.

'I can do it,' he said, but she could feel he wasn't resisting her. There was some strength in his legs, it seemed, though not much and certainly not enough for him to stand up on his own. With an effort she eased him onto the bed, then realized she hadn't pulled back the topsheet first and he was now lying on it.

He chuckled.

'We're neither of us much good at this, are we?'

She tried to smile but found she could not.

'Don't bother about the sheet,' he said. 'I'll lie here for a bit. Can you pass me my pills? And the water?'

She steadied the glass for him as he drank down the tablets.

'Is there anything else you want, Grandpa?'

'Straighten my legs, will you?'

She put down the glass and did as he asked, then stood back and looked over him.

'Do you want me to put that blanket over you?'

'No, I'll be too hot. Just leave it by me. I'll pull it over if I want it. Go and get the painting things, can you? I'll be all right now.'

She bit her lip. It was so difficult to know how best to help him. She felt she should be doing much more than this. The immediate danger seemed to have passed but she prayed Mum and Dad would come back soon.

'I'll get the things,' she said and made for the door.

'Jess?' he called.

She stopped and turned.

'Promise me something,' he said.

She walked back to him and sat on the bed.

'Anything.'

'Promise me you won't tell your mum and dad what's happened.'

'But—'

'Jess, listen.' He took her hand. 'I haven't got long. I haven't got long at all.' He looked her hard in the eyes. 'Do you understand what I'm saying?'

She dropped her gaze and nodded.

'But I want to finish my painting,' he said. 'And I want to finish it here. I don't want to go into hospital, not yet. At the end, maybe, if I've got to, when I've finished my painting. I don't much care what happens to me then. Do you understand?'

She didn't want to understand, and she didn't want to promise to keep silent and bottle all this inside her. She wanted to share it with Mum and Dad the moment they came back; and she felt they deserved to know. They loved Grandpa just as much as she did. But she knew Grandpa would never see it that way.

She said nothing; but nodded once again.

'Go and get the things,' he said.

Struggling to conceal her distress, she ran from the room and out into the sunshine again; and there, standing in front of the cottage, were Mum and Dad.

And a man.

Chapter Six

'This is Alfred,' said Dad. 'Alfred, this is Jess.'

'And that's short for Jessica, isn't it?' said the man. 'I've been hearing all about you and I'm very pleased to meet you. I've got a cat called Jessica. She's not a swimmer like you are but she likes a nice bit of fish.'

And he held out his hand.

Jess was still thinking of Grandpa and felt unprepared for this string of unrelated facts, but she took his hand and hers seemed to disappear inside it. He was elderly, like Grandpa, and seemed friendly enough, if a little eccentric. He was tall and ungainly and had a huge floppy nose which looked like a blob of Plasticine that had fallen onto him by accident. His eyes were bright and direct and reminded her of a child she'd once seen watching a magician.

He looked about him.

'This river's a beauty for swimming and there's a good beach at Braymouth. My sister lives there. Wouldn't live anywhere else, she says. She's got a cat, too, but it's called Jasper. That's funny, Jessica and Jasper, two J's. Now there's a thing.'

And he went on talking about his older brother in South Africa, his other sister and her husband and their four children in London, and why they didn't like living there but had to, and his nephews and nieces and how sorry he was that he didn't have any grandchildren but maybe there was still hope.

Jess looked and listened, feeling somewhat nettled that no one had asked about Grandpa. She would have to interrupt this man soon, if Mum and Dad didn't say something.

Mum smiled at her.

'Jess, you'll never guess. We went to meet Mr and Mrs Gray and ask them if they knew anyone called Alfred and it turns out he's Mrs Gray's father.'

'My son-in-law built this cottage,' said Alfred, quick to regain control of the conversation. 'And he's got more houses round Braymouth way. He's a good lad. Handy with tools. Him and my daughter put a lot of work into these holiday cottages. Not that they ever make much money out of them. They're too honest to be good at business.'

'Spoken like a true cynic,' said Mum.

'Absolutely,' said Alfred, clearly without the slightest idea what she meant. 'Anyway, where is the old boy?'

'He's in bed,' said Jess. She saw a look of alarm on Dad's face and quickly added, 'He's having a rest.'

Dad narrowed his eyes.

'He's been all right, hasn't he?'

'Yes.' She looked away, certain he'd seen the lie in her face.

'I'll go and see if he's awake,' he said.

'Don't disturb him on my account,' said Alfred. 'Not if he's sleeping. No hurry. Haven't seen him for sixty years. Another hour or two won't make much difference. We can stay here and chat till he wakes up.'

Mum and Jess exchanged glances.

'Well, I'll go and check anyway,' said Dad, and he entered the cottage. Mum smiled at Alfred.

'Pop'll be pleased to see you.'

'I doubt that very much,' said Alfred. 'He never had any time for me when we were boys. Don't suppose he'll have much more now. Unless he's changed, and that's even less likely.'

Jess stared at him, stunned by his words. Yet he had spoken them without bitterness or sarcasm, indeed with only obvious affection. She tried to imagine what Alfred must have been like as a boy. Big for his age, that was for sure, and probably much as he seemed now: bumbling, well-meaning, and frustratingly fond of words.

Grandpa would not have wanted to spend much time with him.

'And how's his temper?' said Alfred.

'Short,' said Mum. 'With everyone except Jess.'

'Ah?' Alfred wheeled round and looked Jess over. 'Now I can understand that.'

She felt herself blush but fortunately Dad came back at that moment.

'He's awake but he looks dreadful, really pale and weak, and he's very out of sorts. He didn't even have the strength to snap at me when I tried to straighten the sheets.' He looked at Jess. 'You sure he was OK when he was with you? He says he's just tired but I don't like the look of him. And I thought he wanted to get that painting finished.'

She looked down, unsure of how much she should say.

'He's done some of it but I think it wore him out a bit.'

'So he hasn't finished it?'

'No.'

Dad's face darkened.

'We're in for trouble, then.'

Jess glanced at Alfred and wondered whether they should be talking about Grandpa like this in front of him. But to her surprise he was chortling to himself.

'Reckon I turned up in the nick of time. If he's going to be that bad tempered, he can vent it on me like he used to and I can give you all a break. It'll be like old times.'

'I'm not quite sure we should allow that to happen,' said Dad.

But Alfred only laughed even more.

41

'You needn't worry about me. He was always going for me when we were kids. I used to drive him mad. You see, I don't know whether you've noticed, but I have a sort of a tendency to talk a lot. So they say, anyway. Always have done. But he was—well, he was always wrapped up in his own thoughts. Self-contained, you know what I mean? Trouble was, he was the only other boy for miles around so I used to go and look for him, and spend time with him, you know, for company, which I don't think he always appreciated. So don't worry—I'm used to him giving me a bad time. I never took any notice in the old days and I won't take any now. As I say, it'll be like old times.'

Dad frowned.

'Well, let's hope it doesn't turn out like that. Anyway, I told him you're here. He didn't seem surprised you're still living in the area.'

'Just surprised I'm still living at all, eh?'

'Well, yes, he did say something to that effect. Anyway, he says it's OK to take you through to see him.'

Jess caught Dad by the arm.

'Dad, can I go for a walk?'

'A walk? Where?'

'I want to explore.'

'We've just been exploring and you didn't want to come.'

'That's because I thought I ought to stay with Grandpa. Please, I won't go far.'

'But what about lunch? Alfred's going to be joining us and—'

'I'm not hungry, honestly. I just want to—'

'But I don't want you wandering around on your own.'

'Why not?'

'Well, it's . . . ' He glanced at Alfred. 'I mean, round here . . . anything could . . . '

Alfred read his thoughts as easily as Jess did.

'She should be safe enough,' he said, 'as long as she doesn't do anything stupid or go too far. The only problem in these parts is, if you do get into trouble, there's nobody for miles around to help you.'

Jess thought of her feelings earlier, of the clear sensation of someone's presence; but she said nothing, still determined to go off.

Alfred mused on.

'She should be all right. She looks like a sensible girl. And it's good for walking round here. Bit lonely but I like feeling I've got the place all to myself, even if I do get down in the dumps sometimes when my daughter and son-in-law are out and I've got nobody to talk to. But my sister comes over from Braymouth every Tuesday and Sunday and on Wednesdays we—'

'But what about the river?' said Dad, quick to interrupt before Alfred could get into his stride. 'Jess'll be drawn to that. You said it's good for swimming but is it really safe?'

'Safe enough for a good swimmer. No, the only thing your girl'll have to worry about is boredom.' He winked at her. 'No boys round here.'

She looked down.

'I'm not bothered about that.'

She was desperate now to get away on her own. She needed seclusion to come to terms with her anxieties about Grandpa; and he needed seclusion, too, not the company of a garrulous old acquaintance. He needed to recover his strength and self-confidence so that he could make another attempt on that painting. Even here, away from his presence, she could sense his frustration. And the thought that one more attack might cost him his life and deny him the thing he yearned for filled her with fear.

Dad still looked uncomfortable at the thought of her going off on her own but he argued no further and finally, with some reluctance, went inside with Alfred. Mum lingered for a moment.

'Take a sandwich with you?'

'No, thanks. I just want to—'

'I know. It's all right.' Mum touched her on the arm. 'But be careful, OK?' And she went inside.

Jess stood there, feeling slightly guilty but still impatient to be gone. A desire had been growing in her mind ever since this morning and she knew the time and mood were right for it now.

She ran down to the clearing, packed up the painting things and brought them one by one back to the cottage; then turned the other way and started briskly up the hill.

Chapter Seven

Somewhere up there was the source of the river, Grandpa had said, and she felt a powerful desire to find it. She didn't quite know why. Perhaps, she thought, given her anxiety about Grandpa and the unmentionable thing she was unable to come to terms with, she needed to contemplate the beginning of something rather than the end; to experience something more enduring than human life.

More enduring, even if not permanent. She knew that even these things around her would pass away some day: trees would wither, rocks would crumble, and even the gabbling stream would one day dry up, though she didn't like to think of that.

Yet these things felt permanent; and that feeling gave her comfort now.

Grandpa, of course, would have no time for such musings. He would tell her to take one day at a time, one second at a time, not to think of the future or the past but to live now; to be a warrior of the spirit.

That was how she'd always thought of him: a warrior of the spirit, a man who had always seized life, run with it, invested his whole being in it. And now, at the ebbing of that life, she wondered whether at last he'd granted himself a moment of grace to look back and evaluate what he had done.

Probably not. Probably he would go on living the present right through to the end. And after that . . .

After that was something she didn't like to think of.

After that would come soon enough.

She pressed on up the hill, telling herself as her legs grew heavy that the climb would be worth it for the view alone, even if she didn't find the source. Fortunately there was a path, scraggy though it was, which hugged the stream as far up the slope as she could see; with any luck it would take her all the way.

She stopped for a moment to gather breath, enjoying the melody of the water as it gurgled past her on its way down to the valley she had left behind her. Then, narrowing her eyes, she gazed up the hill again.

The high ground was studded with tall trees whose peaks seemed to claw the skyline as they swayed in the breeze, yet even from here she could see that the soil up there was rockier, the woodland sparser.

She pushed on, thinking of Grandpa again and how he must have come this way as a boy. Perhaps he'd come with Alfred, though, being the loner that he was and clearly as impatient with others then as he was now, she suspected he'd mostly have come on his own. Like her, he had no brothers or sisters and, like her, he enjoyed, indeed needed, his own company. No doubt he'd been the same as a boy.

Yet they all knew so little about his life then. He never talked about it, even to Dad, and, if asked questions, would only mutter the same old response: that there was nothing to tell, that the only reality was now, that the past and future were merely brigands that stole from the present and gave nothing back.

So she didn't ask him about the past or the future or his art or the fire that took away his parents or Dad's mother who died when he was five and whom he scarcely remembered. She kept her mouth closed on all these things, though sometimes she yearned to talk about them.

And once in a while, in more cynical moments, she told herself the only reason he tolerated her more than he did anybody else was because he didn't feel pestered by her, as he so clearly—and unreasonably—felt he was by others.

Yet such moments were rare and usually of short duration. There was something in Grandpa's eyes, something he couldn't disguise and which spoke to her in a way that his words often didn't; and her doubts would recede.

She tramped on up the slope, gauging the distance to the top.

It was still some way and she wondered for a moment whether she should turn back and try for the source tomorrow. Mum and Dad would certainly worry if she stayed out too long.

But the urge to continue was too great. She hurried on, the river still running skittishly past her but the path thinning with every step. A hundred yards further, it petered out altogether.

She stopped and gazed back down the slope. The cottage was far below her now and only just visible by the base of the valley. She glanced at her watch.

Three o'clock; she really should turn back. She stared up the hill again. The ground was much rockier now, yet there was still no sign of an end to the trees, even though she was much closer to the top. The river had narrowed over the last hundred yards but was still strong and fast and loud.

She walked on, unable to resist the pull of the source. The trees seemed to cluster more thickly here and the air was darker, danker, more stifling. She hurried forward, anxious to leave this section behind her. Then, with unexpected suddenness, the trees fell away.

To her surprise she found herself facing a slender gorge with rock rising on either side and a long upland lake stretching several hundred feet before her to an almost sheer face at the end about forty feet high. From the top, splashing down over blanched stones, was a waterfall.

She stared almost in disbelief at the splendour of the sight. This upland lake, she quickly saw, was simply a larger, more muscular limb of the river itself. From where she stood, close to the outlet channel, the ground dipped sharply over hard impervious stones so that the water rushed thirstily away down the slope. The far end of the lake served as a plunge pool for the waterfall.

And the source must be somewhere above that.

She clambered round the side of the lake, trying to check her footing on the uneven ground yet unable to resist gazing at the water. It was clear all the way to the bottom, and quite deep, at least twelve feet around the middle and deeper still at the turbulent base of the fall itself. But towards the outlet of the pool the floor of the lake rose sharply to a shallow, stony lip over which the water gushed on its way down through the trees.

She wandered closer to the plunge pool and saw eddies in the water beyond the torrent where the errant powers of the fall swirled before being drawn into the main thrust of the stream and sucked away down the valley.

She knew she shouldn't linger here—she'd been out far too long already—yet it was hard to tear herself away from this place. There seemed to be a kind of spell over it, just as there was by the cottage; as though everything touched by the river held an enchantment. And her yearning to reach the source grew stronger than ever. It was then that the feeling came back to her.

Someone was near.

Someone was very near.

Once again she could not account for this feeling. She had seen no one, heard no one; yet she found herself turning about, scanning the pool, the rock, the trees. It made no sense: Alfred had said there was no one for miles around. But this only gave her more cause for concern: if there were somebody nearby, and that person turned out to have hostile intentions, she would not be able to expect help.

She clenched her fists and told herself not to be melodramatic. The chances were that anyone round here would be a rambler and no doubt perfectly harmless;

and it was more than likely her instinct was wrong anyway: she was probably alone after all.

Then she saw him.

Standing at the top of the fall, framed against the sky, was the figure of a boy. At least, it looked like a boy, though he was quite tall and it was hard to make out his features against the glare of the sun. He seemed to be wearing nothing but black shorts, but that, too, was difficult to be sure of. She watched and waited, uncertain what to do, and whether she had been seen.

He didn't move, didn't appear to look down towards her, and seemed almost locked there, as though he were part of the stream itself. Indeed, she suddenly realized with a shock that he must be standing not by the side of the stream but in the rushing water itself, at the very lip of the fall.

She stared, trying to see more, but her eyes were starting to water in the sun. She blinked and rubbed them, and stared back.

But he was gone.

She waited for several minutes, watching, listening, wondering. But he did not reappear.

Unsettled and unnerved, she turned and hurried back down to the cottage.

Chapter Eight

She needn't have worried about Mum and Dad. They were closeted, together with Alfred, in the room where Grandpa lay, their attention on him alone.

But she was glad of that: glad for Grandpa because, however much he disliked it, he needed constant vigilance; and glad for herself, too.

She needed to think.

She said nothing about the river boy. Yes, she'd started calling him that, though the words sat uncomfortably in her mind alongside associations with Grandpa's picture.

She didn't stay with them in Grandpa's room but came straight out and sat in the kitchen, eating the rolls Mum had left out for her and listening all the while to the racing stream and the drone of Alfred's voice.

God, the man rambled; but what was really ominous was that he wasn't being stopped. Grandpa must be truly exhausted or he would have cut him in bits by now. It was up to Mum and Dad to do something but they had looked curiously inhibited when she'd put her head round the door. She'd sensed a tension in that room, as though there had been an argument.

If that were the case, she could guess one very likely reason: they'd probably been urging him to let them take him to hospital for a check up or have a doctor called out.

She couldn't blame them for that, whatever Grandpa said about finishing his picture; if he didn't receive the medical care he needed, he might not even start the thing again, let alone finish it.

But he would have refused them, and no doubt rudely, and that might account for the strained atmosphere. On the other hand, it could simply be Alfred's presence that was causing the tension. It was certainly making *her* edgy.

She heard Grandpa's door open, then footsteps, and Mum and Dad appeared with Alfred just behind.

'I'll look in again tomorrow morning,' he was saying, 'and give him a bit of company. Then you and your girl can have a bit of time to look around.'

'That's very kind of you,' said Mum, 'but we don't want to put you out.'

Jess caught her eye and smiled, knowing what she really meant. Alfred blundered on obliviously.

'Oh, it's no trouble, no trouble at all. I'm happy to help out and it gives him someone else to swear at, doesn't it?' Before Mum or Dad could answer, he turned to Jess. 'And did you go somewhere nice?'

She looked down, her mind still on Grandpa and the picture; but most of all, on the boy up at the fall.

'Nowhere special,' she said.

'Did you swim?'

'No.' She hesitated, then looked across at Dad. 'Can I go in and see Grandpa?'

'You haven't eaten very much,' he said. 'Don't you want to finish your rolls?'

'I'm not very hungry. Sorry, I just want to see how Grandpa is.'

'He might be nodding off. I think we tired him out a bit.'

She thought of the state he was in after the attack, and her promise to him, and swallowed the remark she wanted to make.

'I'll come straight back if he's sleeping,' she said, and hurried out before they could call her back.

Grandpa was lying on his back, his eyes closed, but he

51

heard her and opened them, and reached out his hand for her. She took it and knelt beside him.

'Help me,' he murmured, 'help me.'

He said no more and didn't need to. His face seemed depleted of everything except pain. He turned it from her and stared up at the ceiling.

She felt tears start and quickly lowered her face in case he looked back and saw them.

'I'll help you, Grandpa. You know I will.'

It was the picture that was hurting him. She reached out and stroked the top of his head, and he turned his face back towards her.

'It'll be all right, Grandpa,' she said softly.

His eyes misted, but he did not speak.

She found the kitchen empty but saw Alfred through the window, still lingering, only now outside the front door. Mum and Dad were with him, clearly struggling to get away. She wondered how they had contrived to get him out of the cottage in the first place.

Still, he did at least show encouraging signs of intending to leave, though each step away turned out to be a false start as some new item of information occurred to him which he evidently considered indispensable to them.

She watched, wishing her parents could be, just for once, a little less polite. But at last, it seemed, he really was going. He'd taken two good steps from them, then a couple more. Mum and Dad needed no further encouragement. She noted with amusement the speed with which they hurried back into the house before Alfred could think of anything else to tell them.

They were not a moment too soon. They had scarcely closed the door when he turned to call back to them. She smiled to herself, hoping he couldn't see her face at the window; but he turned away again and lumbered off down the lane.

Suddenly she remembered something. Something important. She ran towards the kitchen door and bumped into Mum and Dad coming in.

'Steady, Jess,' said Dad. 'What's the hurry?'

'I've got to ask Alfred something.'

'Sure you've got time for the answer?'

She laughed and they stepped aside; but Dad caught her arm as she passed.

'Jess, I hate to say this, but—'

'I know. Don't bring him back here.'

He smiled, a little shame-faced.

'He's very nice but, you know, a little goes a long way.'

She dashed out of the house, across the clearing and along the lane that twisted up the valley side away from the river. Alfred was only a short way ahead, his gait as slow and ponderous as his speech. But he heard her coming, stopped and turned.

'Miss Jessica,' he said, watching her gravely. Then he winked. 'Thought you'd have had enough of me for one day.'

She looked down, hoping his remark was based on luck rather than wisdom.

'I wanted to ask you something,' she said.

'Ask away. I'm always happy to answer questions if I can.' He chuckled to himself. 'And . . . er . . . sometimes even if I can't.' He took a deep breath to elaborate on the subject but she saw what was coming and quickly cut him off.

'You said there aren't many people round here.'

'That's right. And no fleshpots for the likes of you.'

'No what?'

'Fleshpots. It's all right, I'm only joking. No young people anyway. Different in Braymouth. There's quite a few young people in Braymouth. There's—'

'But there must be some people round here. My age, I mean.'

'Lonely already? And you've only been here a day. I

always said this was no place to bring teenagers. Not unless you've got brothers and sisters, I suppose, or friends. Kids your age don't want to spend their time looking at birds and flowers.'

'You must have done. And Grandpa. When he lived here.'

He stroked his chin.

'I suppose you're right there, though I never thought of that before. But I only really liked it here as a boy when I had company.'

Company meaning Grandpa, she supposed. No wonder the sparks had flown at times; one boy yearning for company, the other solitude. But she was getting distracted from what she had come to find out.

'So there's nobody my age at all round here?'

'Not for miles. Braymouth, like I say—now, they've got a youth club there, and a discotheque, or whatever they call it, and there's a fast food place in the town centre where they all hang out and make a lot of noise. But not round here. Too quiet. Nothing happening.'

She looked hard at him, needing it fully confirmed.

'No boys, then.'

'Boys? No, no boys, like I told you earlier.'

She looked away. She should go now. He had told her all he could and he was probably already jumping to the wrong conclusions about her.

She looked at him again, unsure whether to question him further.

'Do you . . . get lots of ramblers here?' she said eventually.

'Ramblers? No, not many. Round Braymouth there's plenty. They go for the coastal path, see. My sister used to be president of the Braymouth Backpackers Association, before she got too old for it. I never used to go. I'm not one for rambling, myself.'

She stifled a giggle that threatened to escape her at this unintended irony and pressed him further.

'But there must be some people who come walking this way?'

'Not many. We're too remote. We're not on the way to anywhere and there's no village or anything, no pub. That's one thing I've always regretted. No pub. I couldn't have stood this place if I'd been on my own. But my mum and dad only died a few years back, and I had my own wife until last year, and my children, and we all lived here together and worked the smallholding. And then my daughter Megan and her husband came to live with me because they wanted to start setting up these holiday cottages. So you see, I can't complain about being left on my own.' He gave her another wink. 'But I do complain, mind. Naughty, aren't I?'

She glanced towards the cottage.

'I'd better get back.'

He looked at her and smiled.

'All right, Miss Jessica. If you have to.'

She felt a pang of guilt at being so impatient to get away. There was no unkindness in this man. Perhaps she'd been a little hard on him.

But she didn't wait for him to start talking again.

Over supper she tried to think things through.

What Alfred had told her made no sense, yet she was probably making a mystery out of nothing. Just because he hadn't seen many ramblers round here didn't mean there weren't any. And this boy had probably not been alone; maybe he'd had his family nearby, just out of view from where she'd been standing. Perhaps, if she'd climbed up the rockface, she'd have seen them all walking over the hill. They might have been looking for the source, too.

Yet he had looked nothing like a rambler, standing in the stream itself and wearing—she was sure of it—only a pair of shorts; he couldn't have walked far dressed like that so either he and his family were living in or renting a place nearby—which wasn't possible according to Alfred—or they'd driven here to have a walk.

But there was only one road this way, the tiny lane that straggled over the valley peak to Braymouth. And she'd seen no car.

She glanced across the kitchen table at Grandpa, slowly chewing his food as he sat slumped in the wheelchair. At least there were no more arguments about that now, though she knew what it cost him to have others push him about.

Mum spoke.

'You all right, Jess? You're very quiet.'

She saw Grandpa's eye flicker towards her.

'I'm fine,' she said quickly. 'Just thinking.'

'OK.'

He held her gaze a moment longer, then turned back to his food.

After supper they wheeled him through to the sitting room and watched television, but she could tell, as she glanced at him throughout the evening, that his mind was elsewhere. The unfinished picture sat in the corner of the room, propped against the wall, mutely speaking to her; and the fact that he'd turned his back to it and refused to give it his attention only proved to her how much he cared about it.

Unlike him, she found herself gazing at it constantly, so much so that by the end of the evening, though part of her had somehow watched the television and even answered questions from Mum and Dad, it was as though her whole being had been centred in unbroken meditation upon the picture; and on the mystery of the river boy.

By the time she went to bed, her belief in the boy up at the fall had faded; and only the mystery remained.

Chapter Nine

But in the night she saw him again.

The river roused her from a restless sleep, and she rose and went over to the window and gazed out over the moonlit clearing.

A figure was moving in the stream.

She stiffened and stared. The features were smothered in darkness but there was enough moonlight to show her what she needed to see.

It was the boy from the fall.

The river boy.

She edged to the side of the window but he did not glance her way. His attention was all on the stream. He walked slowly, clad, she now clearly saw, only in shorts, his head bowed as though he were studying the water.

She stared, half in wonder, half in fear. Who was this boy? What was he doing out in the river in the middle of the night?

He glanced towards the window.

She drew back, out of sight, and waited for a few moments; then, unable to resist, slowly peered round again in time to see him disappear from view around the side of the house as he followed the stream down towards the lower ground.

Suddenly she was hurrying down the stairs. She had to settle this mystery once and for all, had to ask this boy who he was, what he was doing, why he was here. He didn't look dangerous. There was no reason why she shouldn't speak to him. But she would keep herself hidden, until she was really sure of him.

She struggled into her coat and fumbled with the key to the front door, hoping the sound would not carry. It turned at last and she slipped out of the cottage and across the clearing towards the stream, clutching her nightie around her knees.

But there was no sign of the boy.

She stared about her, breathing hard. This didn't make sense. He couldn't have walked more than a few yards in the time it had taken her to get here, and there was enough moonlight to see him by.

But all she saw was the river flowing past her, giving no sign that anyone had ever travelled through it. She pulled her coat around her, feeling suddenly strangely vulnerable; then she tensed.

A figure was walking towards her.

But it was only Dad.

To her surprise, she found herself running towards him.

'Jess,' he said softly.

She threw her arms around him and he held her, not speaking for some time, just stroking her hair. Then, after a few minutes, he kissed her head.

'What's going on?'

She drew back and looked up into his eyes.

'I don't know. I . . . I don't understand what's happening to me. It's this place, I think. It's like . . . '

'Like what?'

'I don't know. Like there's a presence here. I felt it when we first arrived.'

'A ghost, you mean?'

'I don't know. Nothing nasty—I don't mean that but . . . '

She bit her lip, knowing she couldn't mention the boy. Dad never had much time for what he called 'cranky ideas', by which he meant anything science had yet to explain. But he wasn't making fun of her and she was glad of that.

'I know what's really upsetting you,' he said. 'It's Grandpa, isn't it?'

That, at least, was partially true. She nodded and tried to look cheerful.

'I'll be all right now, Dad.'

'Let's go inside.'

They walked back to the cottage, arm in arm.

'What's the betting your mum hasn't woken up?' he said.

'She must have done with all the noise I made waggling the key, and then you coming out after me.'

'So what's the betting?'

She stopped and thought for a moment.

'You get me a decent desk lamp.'

'And if I win?'

She thought again.

'I'll clear my junk out of the utility room.'

'You're supposed to have done that anyway.'

'Well, I really will do it. The moment I get home.'

'Done.'

They shook hands on it and went in, and at once there was a shout. But it was Grandpa calling from his room.

'What's going on? All that rushing about.'

'Nothing,' called Dad. 'Everything's fine. You OK?'

Grandpa muttered something but didn't speak again, and after waiting for a few more moments to make sure he was all right, they climbed the stairs. Dad put his head round the door to the main bedroom, then looked back at her.

'The utility room. You owe me.'

'Evidence.'

He laughed and pushed the door open to reveal Mum lying fast asleep, as relaxed as a child, one arm dangling over the side of the bed.

'Wish I could sleep as easily as that,' he said. 'And I wish you could, too, my love.'

'I'll be all right now.'

'Well, come in and wake us if you find you're still worrying, OK?'

'OK.'

Back in her room she tried to compose herself for sleep. But the image of the boy haunted her more than ever now and, after a couple of hours of struggle, realizing that rest was beyond her, she gave up, climbed out of bed and wandered back to the window, and leaned there, gazing out into the night.

Chapter Ten

It was dawn before she lay down again and finally managed to sleep, her thoughts drowsily centred on Grandpa and the river boy. When she awoke, she found the sun streaming in through the window and Mum sitting on the bed.

'Jess, Dad's just told me about last night. What happened?'

Jess yawned and Mum quickly spoke again.

'Don't tell me now if you're still sleepy. We can talk later.'

'No, it's all right.'

She rubbed her eyes, trying to think what to say. She was clear in her mind that she wasn't going to mention the river boy to anyone, at least not until she knew more about him. Right now she wasn't even sure he really existed. Besides, Mum and Dad had enough to worry about with Grandpa; the last thing they wanted was her causing concern as well.

'I don't really know what happened,' she said finally. 'It's like I said to Dad — there's something strange about this place.'

'Something spooky?'

'No, not spooky, just strange. I suppose it should feel spooky but it doesn't. It just feels like—'

'Like time doesn't exist.'

She sat up.

'Yes.'

Mum nodded.

'I've felt it, too. I know what you mean. It's like we're

caught in a sort of time warp. Maybe it's just us. We're used to city life and we see change all the time. But this place probably hasn't changed much for hundreds of years, certainly not since Pop was a boy.'

'He said it felt different.'

'Well, it probably does to him. I expect that's because he last saw it as a boy and now *he's* changed. His feelings about life will be different compared with then. I don't suppose the place itself has changed much. That's probably why it feels timeless to us.'

Jess lay back in bed again, thinking.

'Do you want to go home, darling?' said Mum. 'We can, you know.'

'No, we mustn't. We've got to stay, for Grandpa's sake. Anyway, I like it here. Really.'

Mum sighed.

'Well, we did plan it for Pop's sake but if you really were unhappy, I'd put my foot down with him and take the consequences. And I know Dad would back me up. We both feel guilty enough as it is, being so bound up with Pop. You must think we're neglecting you and we probably are.'

'I don't and you're not. We don't need to go. I just had a . . . sort of . . . funny moment, that's all. You don't need to worry about me any more. We've got to put Grandpa first. And please don't tell him about last night if he asks you anything. He called out when we came back into the house but I'm hoping he was half-asleep and won't remember it.'

Mum squeezed her hand.

'All right, we'll stay, but if you do find this place makes you uneasy and you want to go home, we'll pack up and go the same day. OK?'

'You won't need to.'

'But is it OK?'

'Yes, Mum, it's OK.'

'Anyway, since you mention Grandpa, there is something I wanted to talk to you about.'

'The picture.'

'Yes, and his health. You must have noticed how much worse he's got during the last twenty-four hours. Well, while you were out walking yesterday, Dad and I tried to persuade him to let us take him home so that he could go back to the hospital. They know him there.' Mum rolled her eyes. 'My God, they know him. Anyway, we thought he'd be more comfortable in the hospital back home. It's a nice place and everyone's very friendly. Well, he was having none of that so we tried Plan B.'

'The hospital at Braymouth.'

'Right. It's only small, so Alfred says, but at least it's better than watching him waste away here, getting more and more fractious. Well, we got an even worse response with that suggestion. He doesn't even want us to call out a doctor. Says he'll refuse to see anyone.'

'So what are you going to do?'

'I've told him we'll give him another twenty-four hours and, if he's no better, then I'm going to call a doctor out whether he likes it or not, though I don't envy the poor devil who gets lumbered with the job of coming and having his head bitten off. Anyway, if Dad and I were a bit tense yesterday, that's why.'

So she'd been right. But they should have known Grandpa would fight against going into hospital; and no doubt he didn't want to see anyone because he knew the doctor would only argue the same way as Mum and Dad.

'Then there's this painting,' Mum went on. 'He's so strung up about it but he won't tell us anything. I can see you know more about it than we do—as usual. I suppose I ought to feel jealous that he tells you things he won't tell us but I'm glad he trusts you. He needs to trust somebody.'

She shrugged.

'Anyway, as I see it, considering the state he's in, what matters now is that we give him every chance to finish the painting—if we can keep Alfred from driving him bananas first. If he can just finish the thing, maybe he'll get some peace of mind.' She frowned. 'And be able to accept what has to come.'

Jess gazed up at the window and listened to the dancing stream.

And maybe I will, too, she thought.

She set Grandpa up by the river in the same spot as before, but this time in the wheelchair, which he now seemed to have accepted without complaint. Mum and Dad, as secretly agreed with her, were stationed out of sight above the cottage ready to intercept Alfred on the lane and steer him to the kitchen for coffee.

She made sure Grandpa had everything he needed, then wandered a few yards down the bank, keeping carefully in sight while she waited to find out whether he wanted her by him or just somewhere within hailing distance. Sometimes he liked to have her close by but usually he was content just to know she was around, as long as she didn't move about too much and distract him.

She hadn't gone far when she heard him call. She turned at once and ran back towards him, trying to look cheerful. But it was hard: he looked so withered now, like a piece of flotsam thrown up on the beach; even the flame in his eyes had dimmed, as though during the night he had aged another twenty years. He sat hunched in the chair, as still as a sculpture, and the brightness of the sun served only to highlight the pallor of his cheeks.

'Sit with me, can you?' he said.

She sat down in the usual spot, just in front of him and with her back to the easel so that he knew she couldn't see the painting until he was ready to show it; and she waited for him to start.

For some time she heard nothing. That was normal enough: sometimes he would gaze into space for several minutes, or sit there with his eyes closed, mulling over the vision he hoped to translate onto canvas; and that could take time. But this silence went on far too long and she knew something was wrong.

She looked round and saw him weeping soundlessly, tears teeming down his face. She knelt by his side and took his hand.

'I can't do it,' he said. 'I can't do it.'

'You can, Grandpa.'

'I can see the picture in my head. It's so clear. But I . . . I can't . . . '

He was struggling to breathe and soon stopped trying to talk. She waited for a few minutes until he had calmed himself.

'It'll come, Grandpa,' she said. 'It always does. You know it often takes you a while to get started. Like that abstract you did, the one in the front room, remember? And the one of the old church. And what about the girl on horseback? It took you ages before you really got going on that one.'

He looked at her, his eyes still moist.

'You don't understand. It's not my mind that's the problem.' He looked down. 'It's my hands.'

'Your hands? What is it? What can I—?'

'I can't move them very well. It hurts me when I lift the brush. No, don't get your mum and dad. Please, stay here with me. I'll be all right in a minute. I just . . . I just don't know how much strength I've got left in them, that's all. I suppose I'll have to put up with it and try my best.'

He breathed out hard, then glared at the picture.

'Not that this load of trash deserves any more effort. It must be the worst thing I've ever done.'

She looked at the painting and once more felt her mind drawn into the mysterious waters he had conjured with such exquisite skill; and she found herself thinking of the river boy again—both the boy she had seen and the boy she yearned to see, here, before her eyes. She'd

65

been hoping Grandpa would paint him in today; but that hope was fading.

'I still like it, Grandpa,' she said.

'You would,' he muttered, not unkindly, then slowly and painfully he reached for his brush again. 'Go on, buzz off.'

'I thought you wanted me to stay with you.'

'Well, I don't. Go on, I'm all right now.'

'I'm happy to stay, Grandpa.'

'No, you're not. Your mind's on swimming and I don't blame you. It's good weather for a dip. Go on, get lost. I'll shout if I need you.'

And without another glance at her, he started painting.

She watched him for a moment. He wasn't all right— he was anything but all right—and the exaggerated frown of concentration he had adopted in order to get rid of her was far from convincing. Yet he had certainly penetrated her thoughts: despite her concern for him and her preoccupation with the river boy, she had indeed been thinking of swimming.

She wandered a few yards from him, then glanced back. The frown on his face was gone, his mouth had dropped open, his eyes were remote: he was truly absorbed at last.

She smiled to herself. He was so easy to read, so easy to love—for all his faults. She tried not to wince as she saw how much the movement of the brush hurt him.

'Aren't you swimming yet?' he called, not looking at her.

He had spoken lightly but she knew she was putting him off by hanging around.

'I won't be far away, Grandpa.'

He grunted something but didn't speak. That was another good sign: he was getting more and more engrossed. Perhaps he would finish the painting after all today.

He coughed suddenly.

66

She knew what that meant and there was no time to be lost. She pulled off her T-shirt, kicked off her shoes, straightened her swimsuit, and ran away.

She followed the curve of the bank, searching for a spot where the water was deep and clear and good for diving. The river looked so different from here compared with yesterday when she had swum this stretch. Already the woodland was starting to cut her off from the water, though there was something of a path that tracked the meander of the river, albeit some feet back from the bank.

She glanced to the right and saw, twisting among the trees above her, the little lane climbing up the side of the valley on its way to Braymouth. Somewhere over that brow was Alfred's house, the one he had lived in all his life, and no doubt would never leave.

She stopped and looked behind her. The trees and the bend in the river had snuffed Grandpa from view and she wondered for a moment whether she should go back and check he was all right. She shouldn't go too far anyway, in case he called her.

She stiffened suddenly.

There it was again, that feeling of someone's presence, just like yesterday when she had sensed someone and then seen the river boy at the top of the fall.

She gazed about her but saw only trees and, through them, the river flowing by. There was no sign of anyone. She waited for a few minutes, standing as still as she could, just letting her head move as she watched and listened.

Nothing.

She walked on, uneasily, past the clearing she had swum to yesterday morning, and back into the trees again, feeling less exposed here than by the bank. The river had widened to about forty feet and both sides of the valley were now densely wooded.

She came to another clearing and walked down to the water's edge. It was perfect for diving, yet the feeling that someone was near now held her back.

She noticed a tree stump close by and stood on it. From here she could see the texture of the river more clearly. The current was quite strong and the ground shelved quickly below the bank.

It was a perfect spot to dive. There were no reeds to bother her, the depth was fine, everything was right. She looked about her again and still saw no one.

This was getting ridiculous: she could stand here all day and not see anyone, and end up not swimming at all. She clenched her fists and made ready to dive.

Then heard a splash nearby.

She jumped off the stump and hurried in among the trees, angry at herself for retreating but unable to stop herself. There was a sound of more splashing, then silence. She drew back further from the bank and scanned the river.

Suddenly a swimmer broke the surface.

It was the boy from the fall—she was certain of it. He must have dived in somewhere to the right of her; and he must have swum under water—against the current— at extraordinary speed to come up here.

He showed no sign of having seen her.

He dipped his head and started to swim upstream with a strong, impressive crawl. She crept forward, keeping as low to the ground as she could and trying to catch a glimpse of his face. But all she saw was black, untidy hair, matching equally black, untidy shorts.

It was him, it was definitely him, and he swam like a fish, every bit as well as she did, if not better, though she didn't like to admit that to herself. There seemed nothing he couldn't do: backstroke, breast-stroke, butterfly—he changed effortlessly from one to the other, as though flirting with the water as he swam on against the current. Then, suddenly, he stopped, turned over on his back, and let himself float back down towards her.

She watched, trying once again to see more of his face but he was too far upstream, still floating with the current back towards the place where he had started, and where she still waited, crouched among the trees.

She moved further back among the foliage as he drew nearer but kept her eyes upon him. He seemed unconcerned about where the river was taking him; his gaze was fixed on the sky, his body easy and relaxed as though he were lying on a bed, and his arms made not the slightest motion to propel or steer him. He seemed at one with the water, a creature spawned by the river itself.

Then, just as she thought he might come close enough for her to see his face properly, he turned and dived.

The water seemed to enfold him. She caught a glimpse of his body slipping beneath the surface like a blade, heading downstream; then the trees cut him from view.

She hurried to the water's edge and leaned out, watching to see him come up. But he did not. She craned over the water, scanning the surface as far as she could.

But there was no sign of him.

Suddenly she heard a shout.

'Help!'

She whirled round. It came from Grandpa's direction, but it was not Grandpa calling.

It was Alfred.

She plunged into the trees, racing as fast as she could. The ground, so soft and grassy on the way out, now felt hard against her bare feet. She drove herself back towards the cottage, thoughts of the river boy pouring out, thoughts of Grandpa pouring in.

There was the clearing, and the easel and paints, and, by the bank, Alfred, peering down at the water, the wheelchair by his side.

Empty.

'Grandpa!' she shouted.

There was no sign of him; and the picture was gone, too.

She saw Mum and Dad running towards them from the cottage. Alfred turned to face her.

'Where's Grandpa?' she snapped.

'I don't know,' he said, clearly startled at the fierceness of her manner. 'I just got here and saw the empty wheelchair by the water. I was just having a look to see if—'

Dad arrived, breathlessly, Mum close behind him, and marched up to Alfred.

'Where's Dad?' he said bluntly. 'And how come we didn't see you on the lane?'

Alfred, now looking distinctly hurt at his reception, cleared his throat.

'Well, I took the short cut down from the ridge there. It's a nice little walk when the weather's good and . . . anyway, I saw the old boy sitting by the easel and thought I'd come down this way to join him. Well, I lost sight of him when I got in among the trees and when I came out again into the clearing, he was gone and so was the picture. Then I saw the wheelchair by the edge of the water and I thought maybe, you know . . . '

Dad strode to the bank and gazed over the river.

'What's he done? What's the stupid old fool done? He didn't come back to the cottage. I'm damn sure we'd have seen him. We were right by it.' He shot a glance at Jess. 'I thought you were supposed to be with him.'

'I was but he wanted to be alone to paint and said I could go swimming.'

'But you don't look as though you've been swimming.'

'I didn't go in. I just wandered downstream for a bit. Then I heard Alfred.'

'Well, go in now, can you? See if you can . . . ' He stopped for a moment, breathing hard. 'See if you can find anything. Go down with the current for a bit. If he really has done something stupid, he'd have . . . ' He stopped again, then turned abruptly away. 'We'll check out the cottage in case we missed him. Alfred, can you hang around here and keep an eye out?'

'Yes, to be sure, I can do that. I can—'

But Dad and Mum were already running back towards the cottage. Jess didn't wait either but ran to the bank and threw herself in the river.

The ground was too shallow for safe diving but she was ready for the crunch of the bottom against her and had hands poised to push herself quickly up. She broke the surface and splashed out to the centre of the river.

Go with the current, Dad had said.

She forced her fears aside and focused her mind on the task before her, praying she would not find him here. She knew how much the painting mattered to him and that his frustration was at fever pitch. And then the business about his hands. If he'd tried and failed again to paint, if he'd suddenly felt he would never finish this work, his despair would be overwhelming. He might indeed feel life was not worth living. And with the river so near . . .

She pushed these thoughts aside and drove herself down the river, keeping her head above the water as she looked about her. There was no sign of him here and she prayed again that she would not find him.

After a few minutes she stopped and trod water, searching the banks. Still nothing. To her surprise, she found images of the river boy pressing themselves into her mind again; the boy she had seen only moments ago, swimming this same water.

She started to shiver.

Everything was starting to feel strange, dark, terrifying. She saw images of a boy who appeared where there should be no boy; and images of a painting where a boy should be but was not; and she saw Grandpa, the thread upon which this paradox seemed to hang—but where was he?

He couldn't have thrown himself in the water. He was surely too strong in his mind for that, no matter how desperate he might be. More anxious than ever, she swam back to the clearing and hauled herself out onto the bank.

Alfred was still standing there.

'Have you seen him?' she said breathlessly.

'No, and your mum and dad don't seem to have found him back at the cottage. Well, I'll stay here a bit longer if you want to run down and speak with them.'

She dashed back to the cottage and found Mum round the side, hunting among the trees.

'I couldn't find him,' she said.

Mum looked round.

'How far did you go?'

'Couple of hundred yards downstream. I don't think he'd have gone further if he'd . . . ' She looked away, feeling tears start.

Mum hurried across.

'Easy now. Don't let's worry unnecessarily. It might not mean what it seems. You know what he's like. He might have decided to walk off somewhere. It wouldn't enter his mind to tell any of us. He'd just go.'

'But he can hardly stand up.'

'When has something like that ever stopped him doing what he wants? Well, he's not in the house. Have a look upstream, can you, in case he's wandered up that way.'

'Where's Dad?'

Mum nodded to the trees on the other side of the stream.

'Having a hunt round there. I can't believe he came this way though. I don't see how he could have got up here without Dad or me seeing him. We were just up there, watching out for Alfred.'

'Well, you missed him, too.'

'I know. We had our eyes glued to the lane so I suppose it's possible we could have missed Pop if he came this way. But it still doesn't explain where he is now. Oh, God, here's Alfred.'

Jess turned and saw him lumbering up to join them.

72

'I was just wondering,' he said slowly, 'should I maybe head back and get my daughter and son-in-law to come and help? More eyes the better, I'd say. And we might just—'

'No.' Mum interrupted him quickly. 'It's very kind of you but we'll wait a bit before we do anything like that. We know where you are. We can always drive down to your house if we need any extra help. I'm still hoping he'll turn up.'

'Yes, well, you know where I am. I always think in situations like this—'

'Thank you, yes, but excuse me, we must keep looking.' Mum smiled briefly 'We're very grateful to you for helping and, of course, we'll let you know if we find him.'

'Yes, well . . . ' Alfred's face clouded and he clearly had more he wanted to say, but Mum was already wandering off along the side of the stream.

Jess wanted to go with her but, for a reason she could not explain, she suddenly felt concerned about the feelings of this old man. It didn't make much sense; she knew well enough that she shouldn't give him any opportunity to talk, especially when time was so precious. Yet, in spite of herself, she took a step towards him.

'What was it you were going to say?' she said.

His brow cleared and he looked almost startled to receive such an invitation. And, as if by way of not wanting to abuse her trust, he gave her the concisest answer she could have imagined him capable of.

'He used to love a bit of mischief.'

She stared at him, trying to work out what he meant while she waited for his inevitable elaboration; but he said not a word more and simply ambled off across the clearing and out of sight along the lane.

A moment later, she heard a voice.

'Has he gone?'

She drew breath. It was Grandpa's voice, hoarse and

73

tired but unmistakably his. She looked around her but there was no sign of him.

The voice came again.

'Are you blind or something?'

'Where are you?' she called.

The only response was a laugh.

She stared about her in frustration. She felt it should be easy to gauge the direction of the voice but somehow the sound of the river seemed to distort everything. She ran her eyes over the cottage, the trees, the river, the lane.

No Grandpa.

His voice called out once more, with gentle mockery.

'And there was me thinking you always knew what was in my mind.'

She snorted and called back.

'I'd have to be out of my own mind to do that.'

And she heard him laugh again.

It seemed to come from near the cottage but still she could see no one. She took a few steps towards the front door and waited there, still listening. He had not spoken again, but she sensed she was close.

She stamped her foot.

'Grandpa, where are you? And what are you doing?'

'Getting some practice,' came the answer, and this time Grandpa's sense of the ridiculous gave him away. She ran round the side of the cottage and looked down.

There was the coffin, its lid still on, looking exactly as when they had left it after emptying out all the things.

'I suppose you think this is funny,' she said.

There was a moment's silence, then the lid rose a fraction and two eyes peeped out; and they were laughing. She bent down and opened the coffin fully.

He lay there, clutching the picture to him, his body twisted somewhat to fit himself into the space. His eyes sparkled a moment longer, as though he were proud of his joke; then the light suddenly dimmed.

'Get me out of here,' he muttered.

74

She reached down and tried to help him up, but he was too heavy. And he had no strength of his own left now. She shook her head.

'Grandpa, why did you have to do this?'

He lay back again and looked up at her.

'I saw Alfred coming over the ridge and couldn't face the prospect. So I thought I'd get myself out of the way for a bit until he'd gone.'

'How come Mum and Dad didn't see you? They were just up on the lane.'

'Easy as pie to get past them. They were looking the other way. Anyway, I didn't come across the middle of the clearing. I went through the trees down by the river where they couldn't see me so well and then came back on the cottage from the other side.'

She looked at the picture but he quickly shook his head.

'Don't ask about the picture. I haven't finished it. I can't. My hands and arms are hurting too much. And seeing Alfred coming was the last straw.' His face darkened suddenly. 'I don't feel very well,' he said.

He'd exhausted himself completely and slept through the afternoon. Jess sat at the kitchen table, playing patience, while Dad and Mum read magazines. She felt an air of waiting over them all.

Waiting for Grandpa to wake up; or perhaps to fall into that final sleep from which there was no waking. She didn't know. He snored as he slept, an uncomfortable honking sound that seemed to pervade the whole cottage and take away all restfulness. Yet still, mingled with the snores, she heard the tinkling river, the ever-present music she had come to listen for, constantly.

In the evening, Alfred came again, clumping in through the door, his large head almost touching the lower beams of the cottage. He asked no questions about Grandpa's reappearance but simply said he was glad there had been no accident; then he sat down with Jess at the kitchen table and played cribbage with her, and they all went on waiting for Grandpa.

At eight he awoke and, to her slight embarrassment, called for her alone.

She went through and sat down by the bed. He reached out with difficulty and took her hand.

'Stick with me tomorrow. I've got some idiot doctor coming out to see me and he's bound to try and make me agree to go into hospital.'

'You should go into hospital.'

'Don't you start.'

'But you should. You know you should. It might not be for very long, just to get you over the worst.'

'If I go into hospital, I won't come out again. Except as a corpse. Your mum had no right to ring the hospital.' He closed his eyes. 'Is that Alfred's voice I can hear?'

'Yes.'

'Then you'd better bring the old fool in. Seeing as he's hobbled all this way again.'

'Why don't you like him? I know he talks a lot but he's nice, really.'

Grandpa opened one eye and glanced at her.

'I like him well enough, but I'm not telling *him* that. Go on, bring him in or they'll think I'm being difficult again.'

He *was* being difficult again but she said nothing, fetched Alfred and left the two of them together. Dad had made some soup and she sat down at the kitchen table again, cleared the cards away, and drank it in silence, aware of Mum and Dad watching her. After a while Dad spoke.

'What's on your mind, Jess?'

She looked across the table and tried to organize her thoughts.

There were so many images in her mind now, so many strange feelings she could not come to terms with; and all of them, in one way or another, centred on Grandpa.

'Don't tell us anything you don't want to,' said Dad. 'Just tell us you're OK.'

She saw the anxiety on his face and quickly answered.

'I'm OK, really. Please don't worry about me. I've just got lots on my mind.'

Something was drawing her, she didn't know what; something deep, something powerful, drawing her as irresistibly as the river itself was being drawn into the sea. She looked away, hoping they wouldn't question her further.

Mum stood up.

'I'll just see if Pop can manage a bit of soup.'

'You'll have to spoon-feed him,' said Dad. 'He's hardly got any strength left in his hands. And Alfred might like some. We've got enough, haven't we?'

'Think so. I'll ask him anyway.'

She left and Jess looked across at Dad. He was gazing out of the window towards the river, his lips tight, his eyes narrowed, as though he had seen something outside. She thought of the river boy and quickly looked, too.

But all she saw was the river.

As always.

She reached out to touch him—but stopped and drew her hand back, unseen, and rested it, with her other hand, on the table; then she lowered her head into the cradle of her arms, closed her eyes and listened once more to the tumbling waters.

And the pictures in her mind seemed to tumble with them, onwards and away to a place beyond thought.

Chapter Eleven

In the night she stood at her bedroom window and looked for the river boy again. But all she saw was the dark shoulder of the hill, and the trees, and the stream, sparkling under the stars.

Perhaps she would not see him tonight; perhaps she would never see him again. That might not be a bad thing: his appearances were too uncanny to be comforting. Yet she knew she was deluding herself in this and that, deep down, for some reason she did not comprehend, she yearned to see him. He was part of the mystery of this place.

Perhaps the whole mystery.

She listened to the ripple of water outside, then, after a moment's thought, tiptoed downstairs, brought Grandpa's picture up from the sitting room and held it to the moonlight by the window.

It seemed more unfathomable than ever, this unfinished river scene: without the boy it was but half a picture, half a dream; and destined surely to remain only that. He wouldn't finish it now. He could barely lift a spoon to his mouth. He wouldn't manage more than a stroke of the brush.

If that.

Somehow she felt it was her fault. If she'd only stayed with him instead of running along the river bank. Just because he'd told her to leave him and go swimming didn't mean it was the right thing for her to do, and if she'd stayed, maybe she could have stopped him hobbling off at the sight of Alfred and draining further the meagre reserves of strength that now dribbled from him like sands through an hourglass.

She frowned.

This was stupid, blaming herself when it couldn't make things better. She looked over the picture again, straining to see all the details yet not wanting to switch on the light; and, for a strange moment, the painted image of the river seemed almost to merge in her mind with the real river flowing outside her window.

She felt a gust of cool air and shivered.

What was happening to her? Everything she saw, heard, felt, now seemed but an illusion, a play of senses and impressions, interwoven like a tapestry of visions— pictures unfinished, like the one she now held with such desperate tenderness.

She caught a movement outside the window and stiffened.

Once more a figure was moving in the stream.

She clutched the painting to her and stared, her eyes fixed upon the shadowy form. It was him. There was no doubt about it. Who else could it be, out there, alone in the night? It was almost as though he were wading down the stream purposely for her to witness it.

He stopped and his face turned towards her, and moonlight fell upon it; and, in that instant, she felt he saw her. Yet the face turned quickly away before she could collect herself, leaving her with only a confused memory of it.

He was moving again, always in the stream, wearing, as before, only the same black shorts. The next moment, he had passed from view around the side of the house.

She leaned against the window-sill, clutching the painting, trying to build up courage; then she put it down and hurried from the room.

This time no one must hear her leave the cottage— especially not the river boy, wherever he was now. She reached the foot of the stairs, stopped for a moment, and listened. There was no sound of footsteps, no voices calling after her. She took her coat from the peg and pulled it on over her nightie, turned the key—this time without difficulty—and stepped into the night.

The air was balmy, the breeze light, and the tree-tops seemed barely to move against the sky. A few feet from her the river ran on, cutting its relentless path through the land, oblivious to day or night, or to her. She gazed about her, searching for the river boy.

He was nowhere to be seen.

She pulled her nightie up a few inches and ran lightly to the edge of the clearing where the car stood, gleaming in the moonlight. There was no sign of him here. He must have passed on to the wider stretch of the river.

She ran down, following the canopy of trees until she reached the larger clearing where the lane twisted off up the valley and the river broadened; where, only this afternoon, Grandpa had tried—and failed—to paint.

And she stiffened again.

There, in the middle of the river, was the boy, swimming down on the current with slow, leisurely strokes. He was some distance from her and moving away fast but she hurried into the trees for further concealment, and watched.

It was difficult not to feel envy at his swimming ability. Every movement he made seemed to have authority, yet there was a wildness, too. He wasn't a trained swimmer, that was obvious—just a natural swimmer, a swimmer of such power and grace, she could only stand and admire.

He turned suddenly and, to her consternation, started to swim back towards her, a strong, steady crawl, cutting easily through the adverse current. She drew back, keeping close to the nearest tree and trying to decide what she would do if he swam all the way to her and started to wade back up the stream. She had intended to try and speak to him but knew now that she wasn't ready.

But he did not swim all the way to her. He stopped about fifty feet down, stood up in the middle of the river, and gazed towards her.

She started to tremble. He must have seen her, the way he was just standing there, watching. Yet her body was behind the tree and only her face could be visible, and that was surrounded by foliage. She forced herself not to make any sudden movement, and gazed back at the figure.

Still he stared in her direction, and still she strained to see his features. She saw the thick black hair she had noticed before, but the face was dark with shadow and he was just too far for her to see him well enough.

And still he did not move. She had stopped trembling now, but her eyes remained fixed upon him as she waited for him to do something. But all he did was gaze towards the tree behind which she stood.

He could not see her. She told herself he could not see her. Yet, as she watched, the conviction grew that he was waiting.

For her.

Still motionless, he stood there, staring towards her, and motionless she stared back, keeping behind the tree.

Then, with a strange, almost reluctant suddenness, he turned, swam away towards the first bend in the river and disappeared from view.

Chapter Twelve

In the morning Grandpa was the colour of death.

Doctor Fairweather arrived from Braymouth, a young man Jess liked and trusted at once, though she suspected Grandpa would eat him alive. Dad took him through to Grandpa, left him there and came back to join her and Mum in the kitchen.

The doctor soon reappeared.

'Your father's gravely ill,' he said to Dad. 'What on earth's he doing here? He should be taken into hospital at once.'

'I hope you told him that,' said Dad.

'Yes, but I couldn't seem to get a reply out of him.'

Dad frowned.

'He's refused to go into hospital.'

'Well, we must persuade him. He's doing himself no good here. He needs proper treatment and constant observation.'

'We've tried to talk him into it but he just refuses. We can't force him to go.'

'No, we can't, but we must try and make him see reason.' To Jess's surprise, he turned to her. 'Can you come with us? The only thing he did say as I was leaving the room was that he wants you there.'

She caught Dad's eye and looked down.

'OK,' she said.

But talking drew only one response from Grandpa. He wasn't going and that was final—and further argument merely served to make that response more colourful.

Doctor Fairweather came every day after that. He

would call around midday and examine Grandpa, then come out and make sure they all understood what they had to do.

To Jess the hours of caring seemed to merge into a single day, a day of endless wakefulness. What sleep she had she barely noticed, any more than she noticed the effect that lack of rest produced in her. She noticed only Grandpa and the welling cloud of despair that had grown around him.

Mum and Dad, she knew, noticed it, too, but none of them spoke much; and Grandpa barely a word. He remained in bed, locked in his thoughts, fading by the minute, it seemed, even as they fed him, washed him, helped him to the loo, gave him his medication; and waited.

She understood his pride but wondered why he still resisted the greater comfort of hospital. What had he to stay for now? The picture would never be finished. He had so little strength in his hands, he would never be able to keep the brush in the air. Besides, he had made no mention of the painting.

Dad, too, was suffering, but in another way, and it gave her pain to see it. She knew how much he needed Grandpa's love, but it had always been withheld from him in a way that it wasn't with her. She watched as he rushed about, doing more work than everybody else, taking care of the difficult things Grandpa was too embarrassed for her or Mum to see.

Yet still Grandpa seemed unable to give him the words or the look she knew he craved. This had always hurt her and, although she'd never heard Dad complain about it or speak ill of Grandpa, she knew he took it badly.

She didn't see the river boy at all now, but then, she didn't go near the river either. She put on her swimsuit every morning but it was more out of habit than anything else. When she managed to snatch some moments away from looking after Grandpa, it was not to swim but to grab what rest she could. Somehow, in the pressing immediacy of his condition and her father's distress, she'd ceased almost to think about the river, or swimming, or the strange boy.

Only the discarded painting drew her mind back from time to time, and then not to its riddle but to its creator, lying stricken on the bed and sighing out his life.

Alfred, too, came every day now, sometimes with Mr and Mrs Gray but usually by himself, and she found him a curiously welcome visitor. His mannerisms no longer irritated her and he took his turn to sit with Grandpa and keep him company. But keeping company with Grandpa was no easy matter.

He had lapsed into a world of almost total silence.

Then, to her surprise, on the seventh day he called her to him. She went in, alone, and drew a chair close to the bed.

'Are you going to talk to me today, Grandpa?' she said brightly. 'Or just carry on being a miserable old buzzard?'

'Miserable old buzzard.'

'Oh, that's OK. I thought something was wrong for a moment.'

She heard him chuckle and it was a good sound—the first she had heard for many days. But it did not last, and the darkness fell quickly upon him once more. She leaned closer.

'Grandpa, tell me what it is.'

He looked away and was silent for so long she thought he was not going to answer. But finally he spoke, though in a voice so low she could barely catch the words.

'It's no good. I'll never do it now. I'd thought . . . hoped . . . maybe if I just rested a bit, my strength would come back and . . . ' He looked back at her. 'You might as well take me to the knacker's yard at Braymouth. I'm not going to finish the picture now.'

She stroked his hand, wanting to squeeze it and

somehow infuse some of her own strength into him; but she let go, anxious lest she hurt him.

She had not thought it would come to this; and, to him, she knew it must be unbearable. Defeat—for that was how he would see it—would cost him more than any physical pain. To be wheeled away into some hospital ward, frustrated, resentful, and thus to die, his work uncompleted, was an end she could never have envisaged for him.

Not that she saw him as she knew he saw himself. To her, the more she contemplated this proud old man at the bitter climax of his life and considered all that he had achieved, so much of it so beautiful, the more she found to admire.

The failings she saw, too, clearly enough. But this man, this man she loved, worshipped almost, now lying here wretched in spirit—this man should not be feeling what she knew was in his heart.

'You're not a failure, Grandpa. You're not.'

'I know what I am.' His voice dropped. 'Tell your dad I'll be ready for the hospital tomorrow morning.'

His face grew impassive and she knew it was a sign of dismissal. She wanted to touch him so much now, touch him, hold him, kiss him; but she knew he would not accept sympathy at any cost.

But the cost to herself, to her unexpressed feelings, was great, too.

She ran from the room, choking back the tears. Mum and Dad were coming in and she brushed past them out of the cottage, ran over to the stream and knelt by the water's edge.

This was the end. He was, indeed, truly broken— something she had never thought she would witness. The painting, so near to completion, might as well never have been started. Indeed, it would have been better for Grandpa if this had been so: every painting he'd ever started had been an obsession with him until he'd managed to tear it out of himself, and now this

85

unfulfilled part of his soul would rot away inside him, colouring the last hours of his life.

She kicked off her shoes, tore off the T-shirt she had put on over her swimsuit, and stepped into the stream. The water was cool and bracing against the noonday heat, but she found little joy in it today.

She waded down to where the river flattened out and stood there, the water up to her waist, gazing over the shimmering body of the river. It was such a perfect day for swimming, warm and windless, and it felt so long since she had been in the river; the water seemed almost to yearn for her.

But her yearning was for tears and they mastered her now. And, as she sobbed, she thought of Grandpa, and his life and his dream flickering away.

Then, to her surprise, she heard a quiet voice behind her.

'Why are you crying?'

Chapter Thirteen

The river boy was standing in the stream, just a few yards away, silently watching her.

She drew breath. She had not heard or felt his approach, but then the racing waters and her own sorrows had so overwhelmed her, she had known little else. She felt a rush of embarrassment at being so unprepared.

He stood there, still in silence, taking in not just her, it seemed, but everything about them as well. She studied the face that watched her from within that shock of black hair.

It was not conventionally good-looking, but it was striking, especially in the way the eyes moved. There was an electric intensity about them which she felt should have been frightening; but there was a tenderness there, too, and he seemed greatly concerned about her.

'Why are you crying?' he said again.

She ran a hand against the driving current and, not ready to open her heart to a stranger, put her own question instead.

'Who are you?'

He opened his mouth to answer; but something inside her—something urgent, something incomprehensible—made her call out to stop him.

'No.' She looked down, more embarrassed than ever. 'Don't tell me who you are.' She dropped her voice to a murmur and spoke again, to herself alone. 'Stay a mystery a little longer. I can't take any more truth right now.'

She looked up and saw he was moving forward. Instinctively she took a step back, but he was only making his way past her towards the deeper water.

She watched, ashamed at having betrayed her nervousness. He was clearly no threat and, if anything, seemed more lost in his own thoughts than in contemplation of hers. He waded to the end of the tree-cover, then turned and called back to her.

'Ask me anything you want.'

She stared down at the water, still struggling with her feelings. She had so many questions she wanted to ask: who he was, where he lived, how he'd learned to swim like this, how he'd suddenly appeared in her life.

And why.

But she knew she wasn't ready for questions; or, at least, she wasn't ready for answers. Deep down she knew this boy was linked to the destiny of Grandpa; and answers meant revelation.

And she was suddenly frightened of that.

He seemed unconcerned by her reluctance to talk and simply eased himself into the water, swam a short way down with the current, then turned on to his back and floated, as she'd seen him do that day she'd watched him in secret from the bank.

How long ago that seemed and how anxious she had been to glimpse him again. Yet here he was, and clearly in no hurry to leave her. She watched him as he lay there in the water, calm and relaxed. He seemed so independent, as though he needed no one in the world, yet when she had been struggling with tears, he had looked at her almost like a brother.

She waded to the edge of the tree-cover and stood there.

'It's . . . ' She hesitated. 'It's because of my Grandpa. Why I was crying, I mean.'

He said nothing but she sensed an attentive stillness in him.

'He's dying,' she went on. 'There's nothing anyone

can do about it and . . . and he's going to die unfulfilled.'

She gazed away down the river.

'He's trying to paint a picture. It's an important
picture. It really matters to him and he can't finish it.
His hands and arms are too weak.'

She felt the tears coming back and quickly wiped her
eyes. The boy rolled onto his front and swam towards
her, his eyes never leaving hers. A few feet from her he
stopped and stood up. They faced each other in the
rushing stream.

'You finish the picture,' he said.

'But I can't paint.'

'*He* can.'

His eyes seemed to burn like fire. She stared back,
confused and a little frightened.

'But I told you, his hands aren't strong enough.'

The fire grew stronger still.

'*You* be his hands,' he said.

She looked away, unable to bear the intensity of his
gaze, and, without quite knowing why, dived. The
smack of water on her face was a welcome shock. She
surfaced quickly, a few feet past him, and started a fast
crawl downstream, keeping her face buried in the water
as much as she could.

She didn't look back to see what he was doing but
kept on, driving herself down with the current. This was
all getting too much: Grandpa close to death and now
the boy with his strange talk. She had to get away, had
to swim, had to do something other than talk and think.

It was some minutes before she stopped and trod
water. To her surprise, she had swum, almost without
noticing it, round the first bend in the river. She turned
to look back the way she had come.

There, only a few feet from her and also treading
water, was the river boy, clearly not the slightest bit out
of breath. He shook the hair from his eyes and spoke to
her again.

'If your grandpa died fulfilled, would you bear his loss better?'

'Yes,' she said, somewhat reluctant to answer him.

'And would he feel better, too?'

'Of course he would.'

'Then help him.'

She frowned, at a loss to know what to say. He swam up to within a yard from her and looked her hard in the face.

'And will you help me, too?'

'You?' She stared at him. 'What do you mean?'

He looked down, his eyes close to the surface of the water.

'There's something I've got to do. Something really important to me. I don't want to talk about it now but it's the biggest challenge of my life and . . . I'm a bit scared about it.' He looked up again. 'Will you help me?'

She looked away, trying to absorb this strange request. He sounded as though he genuinely wanted her help and there was an urgency in his voice which hadn't been there before; but she knew she couldn't make plans of any kind with Grandpa as he was. The boy, though, seemed to understand her worries completely.

'If your grandfather finishes his picture, will you help me then?'

'I don't know,' she said, starting to feel trapped. 'It depends on how he is. I mean, I want to help you but . . . look, I can't promise anything—OK?—but if I can get away, where do you want to meet?'

'Up at the source, the day after tomorrow, at dawn.'

'The source?'

'You'll have to climb the rockface by the waterfall. But it's not difficult if you're careful.'

'But why dawn?'

'It's going to take time—what I've got to do.'

This was getting too mysterious for comfort.

'Listen, I've got to get back,' she said.

'But will you come?'

'I don't know.'

'Promise me you'll think about it at least.'

'But—'

'Just say you'll think about it.'

'OK, I'll think about it. But I'm not saying I'll come, OK? It all depends on Grandpa. And Mum and Dad.'

But he seemed satisfied with this.

'I'll wait for you,' he said.

She stared at him, still feeling trapped.

'Look, I've really got to get back.'

Without waiting for him to answer, she struck out upstream. Once again, she didn't look behind her but she assumed he was following just as he had done before. When she finally stopped, she was a few yards down from the tree-cover where they had met. She put a foot on the bottom, turned and looked for him.

But this time he was gone.

The words of the river boy haunted her through the evening, like snatches of song that would not let her go. She went through the motions of helping Mum with the cooking, peeled the potatoes, cut up the vegetables, drained the rice; yet noticed little of what she was doing. Dad went in and fed Grandpa, then came back, his face dark and grave, and the three of them sat down to eat.

After a long silence, Dad's voice broke in upon her thoughts.

'Jess?'

She looked up and saw him watching her.

'Jess, I'm sorry.'

She forced herself back from the world of her mind to the world of those she loved.

'There's nothing to be sorry about,' she said.

He reached across the table and took her hand.

'I expect you know that Dad wants to be taken into hospital tomorrow. Even he's had to admit it's time. I just wish it hadn't turned out like this. I'd have liked him to have finished that painting before he . . . ' He paused, frowning, and his hand tightened round hers. 'I'm still praying he'll pull through. I just can't bear the thought that . . . ' He paused again, breathing hard. 'But, Jess, listen, I'm sorry I've been so bound up with him. I've hardly taken any notice of you, and I know you're feeling things as badly as anybody, if not worse.'

'There's nothing to say sorry for.' She thought of the river boy again and looked down. 'Dad, do we have to take him to hospital tomorrow?'

'It's what he wants. What else do you suggest? He shouldn't have come out of hospital in the first place but now he's actually asked us to take him in, I'm not going to hold him back. God knows, I don't want to see him go in any more than you do, but I can't bear to see him suffering like he is here. It's for the best.'

Mum spoke.

'Jess, what is it you were thinking of?'

'I don't know. I just—' Yet again the river boy's words came back to her. 'Can I . . . can I spend some time with Grandpa tomorrow morning? First thing? Before you send for the ambulance?'

'What is it you want to do?' said Dad.

She turned and gazed out of the window at the light fading over the river.

'I want to be his hands,' she said.

Chapter Fourteen

In the morning she steeled herself and went to him, alone. He was awake but his eyes were weary as they locked into hers.

'I don't want any breakfast,' he muttered as she put down the tray. 'I'll eat at the hospital. If I can stand the food.'

'You're not going to the hospital today.'

'I am.'

'No, you're not. You're painting today. So you'd better get some breakfast inside you.'

He scowled at her.

'I'm not painting. I can't paint any more. And if I can't paint, I don't want to live. And I'm not hungry either, so you're wasting your time.'

'Stop arguing and open your mouth.' She cut the toast into small pieces, picked one up and steered it towards his face.

'I told you,' he spluttered, 'I don't want—'

He saw the toast coming closer, closed his mouth tight and glared at her. She tutted.

'I'm going to hold this toast here until you open up and eat it like a good boy.'

He eyed it with contempt for a while, then grunted.

'It hasn't got any marmalade on it.'

Keeping her eyes on his and the toast poised before his mouth, she reached for the knife, dipped it in the marmalade and spread it for him. He watched her, with grudging respect, then opened his mouth just enough to let her slide the toast in.

'Stubborn as hell, you are,' he said, chewing slowly.

She reached down and took another piece of toast.

'Wonder who I get that from.'

He ate the rest of the toast in silence, his eyes still on her, as though wondering what she would do next. She reached for the coffee pot.

'I don't want any coffee,' he said. He looked hard at her. 'And I mean it.'

'OK.'

He leaned back in the bed, breathing jerkily.

'What time is it?'

'Eight o'clock.'

'Where's your mum and dad?'

'Still asleep.' She thought of them sitting upstairs as agreed, worrying and no doubt wondering what she was up to. Fortunately, they hadn't pressed her to explain what she intended to do. It was good that they trusted her; and just as well they couldn't see what she was about to do next.

'Right, Grandpa. Get ready.'

He looked up at her.

'What are you doing?'

'Helping you to sit up.'

'But I can't move.'

'Yes, you can.'

'I can't. And I don't want to move. Not till the ambulance gets here.'

'There's not going to be any ambulance today. I told you, you're not going into hospital. Not yet.'

'I am.'

'You're not. You're going to paint today. You're going to sit up properly in bed and you're going to finish that picture. And I'm going to help you.'

'Don't be ridiculous!'

'I'm not being ridiculous. And there's no point in arguing about it. I'm not giving in.'

He was fuming now and she could see he chafed to be rid of her. Desperately she clung to her faith in his will,

94

his anger, his courage and, above all, his love for her: the only thing—as she well knew—that allowed her to get away with this.

'You're going to paint,' she said firmly.

'I told you, I can't move my hands properly. How do you expect me to paint when I haven't got the strength?'

She leaned close and looked him hard in the face.

'But I've got the strength. You can use my hands. And we'll finish the picture together.'

He turned his head away, as though anxious to avoid her gaze, and was silent for a long time; then suddenly he looked back.

'Well, I'm not painting in bed. I never paint in bed.'

'Then I'll put you in the wheelchair.'

He glowered at her.

'God, I've never known anyone so pig-headed.'

'I have.'

'Heaven help the man who marries you.'

'I'll get the wheelchair.'

She hurried out before he could change his mind, fetched the wheelchair from the sitting room and pushed it through to him.

And the first big problem arose.

Dad would have to come down to dress Grandpa and that was the last thing she wanted: she didn't want anyone, not even Mum or Dad, to break Grandpa's mood. Fortunately, Grandpa's natural obstreperousness sidestepped the problem.

'And I'm not having anyone dress me. You can put a blanket over me and that's it. And if I want to stop and come back to bed, then I'm going to, whatever you say.' He drew back from her as she leaned forward to help him. 'And I can get in the wheelchair on my own, thank you very much.'

'Who are you kidding?'

She threw back the sheet, put her arms round him, ignoring his mutterings in her ear, and pulled him gently forward.

'Come on, Grandpa, use your stomach muscles. I'm not doing all the work for you.'

'Bully,' he said, struggling towards her.

It was good that he was abusing her. If he had fight in him for her, then he might have enough for life, too; or at least the painting.

Which perhaps was the same thing.

'You'll kill me before my time,' he said, 'if you keep shoving me about like this.'

'You've been killing yourself anyway lately so what's the difference?'

She eased his upper body towards the edge of the bed, then swung his legs round into the wheelchair.

'Hold on to me, Grandpa.'

She felt his arms flop over her shoulders and try to hold her. There was not much strength there, but some. She prayed he would have enough for what lay before them; and that she would, too, not just to lift his body but, more importantly, his mind—at least enough to get him through this ordeal.

And somehow to overcome her own doubts and hold fast to what she believed to be right for him.

The risk was obvious: the strain of this effort to paint could, quite simply, kill him—here, now, any moment. Yet the more she had pondered the words of the river boy, the more the logic of this course of action had justified itself to her.

Death was already so close; and she felt she knew Grandpa well enough to hazard that he would be willing to risk losing a day or two of a now unbearable life for the chance to die fulfilled.

She sat him at last in the wheelchair and turned it round to face the door.

'Blanket,' he snapped.

She fetched it and draped it round his shoulders.

'No,' he said. 'Over my legs.'

'Your legs?'

'The spindly things at the bottom.'

'No need to be sarky.'

She spread the blanket over his legs and pushed him through to the front door. There was no sound from upstairs but she knew Mum and Dad must have heard them. She prayed they would not come down; if they saw what she was about, they would surely stop things.

But no one called down or appeared on the stairs.

She opened the front door, pushed him outside and closed it behind them.

'Nice day for painting, Grandpa.'

'As long as Alfred doesn't turn up.'

'He's not coming today. He's got to go to Braymouth to see his sister.'

'What a pity.'

She said nothing and pushed him down to the spot by the river where he had tried to paint before.

'I can't paint without my easel,' he said petulantly.

She locked the wheelchair brake, leaned over the top of his head and looked upside down into his eyes.

'And exactly how many times over the years have I forgotten your easel?'

'Well, I was just reminding you.'

She giggled and kissed him on the forehead.

'Grumpy old whatsit.'

She ran back to the house and started to fetch the things, expecting on each trip to see Mum or Dad waiting there, demanding to know what was going on and insisting she stop at once.

But still there was no sound from upstairs.

Ten minutes later, the easel was set up, the picture in place, and everything was ready.

She sat next to him on the put-up chair she had brought for herself and tried to think how to begin. He certainly didn't look ready to paint. His face was so pale, he looked like a ghost, and the more she watched, the more he seemed to be fading from her sight. The only brightness was in his eyes and even that was dwindling.

Yet life still lingered, flickering there somehow, and with it she saw traces of the will power she was counting on, praying for. It would be that, and probably that alone, that would keep him alive long enough to complete this final challenge.

To her relief, though, he seemed at last to be showing some interest of his own in the picture.

'I don't know quite how we're going to do this,' he said slowly, staring at the painting. 'I can't hold the brush very well and I can't keep my arm up without your help.'

'We can do it, Grandpa. Between us.'

'You'll have to be patient with me.' He thought for a moment, then added wryly: 'And I'll . . . er . . . I'll try and be patient with you.'

She smiled.

'And how will you manage that, Grandpa?'

'I won't if you don't stop being cheeky, so shut up and pull the easel closer. How do you expect me to reach it like that?'

She laughed and did as he asked.

'What colour do you want first?' she said.

'Mix me some black.'

'Black?'

He raised an eyebrow at her.

'Do we have a hearing problem?'

'OK, black.'

It was good to banter, good for him and good for her, but she knew the time for joking was now past. She had to let him concentrate. She prepared the black as he directed and waited, wondering what to do next. But he moved first.

His hand struggled forward. She saw what he wanted, reached out and took the brush, and placed it between his fingers. He caught her eye and nodded towards the picture.

'I want . . . I want to work down that right side from the top. Can you . . . can you—?'

'Lift your arm?'

'Yes, and put your hand round mine. I don't think I can . . . '

The brush was slipping from his grasp already.

'I'll do it,' she said.

She sat on the edge of her chair and placed her hand round his fingers to keep the brush in place.

'Not too tight,' he said. 'I can't control it otherwise. That's right. Now, let me get some paint on the brush— that's it—and I'll try and . . . ' He frowned and she felt him trying to raise his arm. 'It's no good,' he said, breathing hard. 'I can't lift the bloody thing.'

'Let me do it, Grandpa.'

Keeping her right hand around his fingers to hold the brush, she slipped her other hand under his elbow and gently raised the arm.

'Is that hurting?' she said.

'A bit but . . . ' He stared at the picture again. 'I might just be able to . . . '

But already she felt him stretch forward, his eyes fixed on the picture with all the desperate intent of a drowning man who spots a slender hope of rescue; and with that intent she felt a trickle of energy run through him.

The brush dabbed at the picture and left its first mark.

'Down,' he murmured, 'I want to go down. No, not that way. Small movements, downward movements. Pull my hand back.' He nodded towards the brush and moved it through the air. 'Like that, see? Little downward dabbing movements. Not too big or we'll mess it up. Come on.'

She steered his hand back to the picture and he continued to paint; and, one by one, the little black tints started to appear, darkening the river scene like feathery black snow. Her arms were aching already and she knew

99

she would have to do something soon, yet she dared not break the flow of his attention.

She thought for a moment, then cautiously propped her left elbow on her leg to take the weight of his arm. There was little she could do for her right arm, and she knew she would just have to bear it.

He seemed to notice none of her manœuvrings. His face had set in that familiar glaze of concentration she had hoped to see. He did not speak now, except to give terse instructions about where to move his hand and what kind of stroke he wanted.

But it was all the same kind of stroke: the little downward stroke, and always black. This was the most puzzling thing. He clearly knew exactly what he wanted, yet with every movement of the brush, the images she had seen were being distorted. The right side of the painting had splashes of black all down it, and now he was working round the top in the same way.

It made no sense; the misty river was still there, clearly visible in the middle of the painting, but the strange dappled effect to the right and at the top changed everything. He finished the top and worked down the left side, still in black, and, after much effort, finished that, apparently to his satisfaction.

She wondered whether he would complete the circle and cover the bottom of the painting with black, too. But, to her surprise, he leaned back in the chair and looked towards her.

'It's finished,' he said.

Three hours had passed and they were both exhausted. She stared at him, then back at the picture which had cost them so much.

And still she saw no boy.

Chapter Fifteen

'It's not one of his best,' Dad said.

He held it up to the kitchen window and studied it with Mum. Jess sat at the table, saying nothing, glad they hadn't reproached her for what she'd made Grandpa go through to produce this; she hadn't realized, until they'd told her a moment ago, that they'd been watching her and Grandpa painting from the upstairs window.

'I think he's ruined it,' said Mum.

Jess instinctively looked round; but there was no danger of Grandpa hearing. They'd put him to bed exhausted and she doubted whether he would wake for the rest of the afternoon. The effort of painting had taken everything he had.

Yet there had been an elation in him as she'd wheeled him back to the cottage, a sense of pride in his voice as he told Mum and Dad that he had finished his picture. He had even talked of feeling better, stronger; but she knew that was wishful thinking. He would sleep now and tomorrow morning they would decide what to do about the hospital.

All that mattered was that he was content, whatever the merits—or otherwise—of the picture.

Mum spoke again.

'I still don't understand why he called it River Boy when there obviously isn't a boy.'

Jess gazed out of the window at the stream. Somewhere out there another boy was waiting; waiting for his own big challenge, whatever that was. The challenge he had asked her to help him with.

She frowned.

There was only one river boy she knew and his being and hers were now strangely interwoven. The more she thought of him, the more his nature seemed to flow through her like the river itself. Yet it was the painting—inexplicable as it was—which had first created in her mind the mystery of the river boy. To the painting he owed his existence. Just as now, in a strange way, the painting—thanks to his urging—owed its life to him.

She did not understand this final outpouring of Grandpa's spirit. Perhaps it was a work of genius for later, greater minds than theirs; or perhaps just the last spluttered vision of a dying man, his brush held up by the hand of a trembling girl.

Late in the afternoon he woke and asked for a little soup. Dad made it and took it through, and sat with him for a while; then came back and called to Jess.

'He's asking for you again.'

She looked up at his face and saw the pain there, and tried to think of something to say; but he turned quickly away and clattered the tray down on the kitchen table. Mum looked him over quizzically.

'I'll go through,' said Jess.

Grandpa lay in his bed, head back, mouth open, eyes half-closed. She reached forward and straightened the pillow which was slipping to the side. He opened his eyes fully and met her gaze, then, with great difficulty, stretched out his hand and took hers.

She knelt beside him and waited to see whether he wanted to speak. For a long time there was silence, punctuated only by slow, uneven breaths, then his lips moved and she caught a whisper of words.

'Thank . . . you.'

He said no more for several minutes, but continued to hold her hand and look into her eyes. Then the mouth moved again.

'I'm so . . . I'm so . . . '

'Don't tire yourself, Grandpa.'

'So . . . proud of you . . . so . . . proud . . . '

'I'm proud of you, too, Grandpa. I'm proud of both of us. I—'

She broke off, seeing his lips quiver. He spoke again, slurring his words slightly.

'Tell me . . . tell me . . . what I can do . . . for . . . you.'

She looked down, trying not to cry, trying not to think that these might be his final hours with her. She had nothing to ask of him, at least nothing for herself. What could she ask for, when he had given her so much? The only thing she still yearned for was to see him show love to Dad. But love could not be fashioned just by the asking.

She looked into his face again.

'Just be happy, Grandpa,' she said.

In the evening he seemed brighter. He joked with them all and talked of feeling better, and of thinking he maybe wouldn't need to go to the hospital at Braymouth after all but would see out the rest of the holiday and then perhaps go home and start living again—only with no more painting, he added: painting was too much like hard work, especially with a slave-driver like Jess pushing him on.

She listened and laughed at his jokes when he wanted her to. It was good to see him happy and relaxed. It did indeed seem as though a burden had lifted from him, and to hear him talking of the future, as though there were a future, filled her with hope. Perhaps he would pull through this after all.

At sunset she walked off alone by the river, down to the place where they had painted together, and she stood by the water's edge and gazed westwards at the fading glow in the sky.

Tomorrow? What would tomorrow bring, and how many tomorrows did he really have? He had talked as though there were many, yet for all her rejoicing at his happy spirit, she saw only one tomorrow. She would live that first, before she thought of any more.

A shiver of cool air wafted over her and passed; and she remembered her debt, and why she had come out. She looked down at the unsleeping river.

'I can't see you, River Boy,' she murmured, 'but I know you're there, whoever you are, whatever you are. And . . . and I think you can hear me.'

She lowered her voice still further and went on, speaking to the river.

'I don't know why I think you can hear me. Maybe I'm just hoping you can hear me. Maybe I'm just hoping there really is some kind of magic about you and you're not just an ordinary boy.'

She stopped, trying to understand her thoughts; but they ran faster than the river itself.

'I don't know why you think I can help you with this thing you're scared of, whatever it is, but . . . I'll come to the source tomorrow at dawn, and do what I can.' She frowned. 'But I won't stay long because I'll have to get back to my Grandpa.'

She stopped suddenly, feeling yet again that strange presence she had sensed before; and, in that moment, she knew she had been heard.

In the night she woke, pressed into consciousness by strange yearnings. She sat up and wiped her eyes, and looked towards the window.

Once again the moon was bright upon the sill, and, as usual, the sound of the river raced through her like a stream of chattering thoughts. She stood up, pulled her dressing-gown on and crept down to Grandpa's room.

The door was open, and she saw the bell that Dad had

put by the bed so that Grandpa could ring if he needed them. But Grandpa needed no one.

He was deep in sleep.

She stood there for a moment, watching him, then slowly and softly walked forward and sat down on the chair by the bed. He did not stir.

She leaned forward until her face was close to his. She had so much to say to him; but she did not want to wake him. Not when he was sleeping so soundly.

She opened her mouth to whisper.

He moved slightly, only a tilt of the head towards her, and she thought for a moment she had disturbed him. But then the breathing resumed its pulse and she knew he was still asleep.

Strange, she thought, watching him: here, close to death, his face now seemed almost childlike, as though he had reverted to his youth. He seemed like a young man again, lying asleep after a hard day working at his studio.

She thought of all the things she wanted to say and fumbled in her mind for the best way to express them. But when she opened her mouth to speak, all that came out was a sigh.

'I love you, Grandpa.'

And she knew that was enough.

Chapter Sixteen

In the darkness before dawn, she scribbled a note to Mum and Dad and left it on the kitchen table.

GONE FOR A WALK. BACK SOON. J.

And stole from the house.

Not that they would see it, she thought; she should be back before they even stirred. It shouldn't take that long to reach the source and see the river boy, and even though he'd said that the thing he was going to do would take time, she was resolved to be back before anyone, especially Grandpa, woke up.

The stars were still visible as she set off up the slope but the darkness was giving way to a grey haze, and she knew she had no time to lose if she were to make it to the source in time for dawn. She hurried up the hillside, picturing as she walked the waterfall gushing down that rocky gorge; and remembering the river boy as she had first seen him, standing at the lip.

Perhaps this was how she would see him today, tall, erect, gazing over the torrent from its most dangerous point, just as Grandpa himself had no doubt done many a time.

But when, after an hour's hard walking, she found herself peering up at the fall from beside the upland lake, she saw no figure standing there.

Only sky, lightening by the minute.

Any moment, she felt, the sun would burst over the eastern peak, as yet cut off from view by the sides of the gorge. She looked over the rockface and studied its surface; then, with some trepidation, started to climb.

It had looked easy enough from further out—she'd seen plenty of cracks and ledges—but half-way up, the handholds ran out. She clung there, scanning the rock on either side of her and trying to fight off the sense of vulnerability creeping over her. The nearest handhold seemed to be a small ledge to the right, close to the fall itself.

She paused, then reached out. After an agonizing moment when she thought she was losing her balance, her fingers slid over the rough extremity of the ledge, and she gripped it, breathing hard; then, with an effort, stretched out her foot, pushed it into a fissure a few feet below her, and hauled herself across the face of the rock.

She was over the plunge pool now and only a few feet from the torrent itself. She waited for a moment, trying not to be frightened by the thunderous sound of the water, then reached up and, to her relief, found there was a large crevice and several more just above it.

The climb was easy now and she quickly clambered up, glad to be free of anxiety. At the top, level with the shining lip of the fall, she saw the ground rising once again, but this time only a few hundred yards. And she knew the source was near.

She scrambled over the rim of the rock and wandered on upwards. The sun was over the cut of the hill now and the sky was growing brighter. The stream had narrowed but still ran down with surprising force.

There was no path at all here but none was needed. As she walked, the rocks grew sparser, the ground mushier, and she saw, as she climbed further, that the stream was now being fed by smaller tributaries which straggled down into it from the higher ground.

But the main stream was clear to see and she followed this, growing more and more impatient, more and more excited, until at last, a few hundred yards further on, she found the source, a marshy area of peat and moss and bog cotton grass, the water bubbling out of the ground and dribbling down the slope in a tiny stream which, though gentle at first, quickly cut a channel through the soft soil and grew in power and energy and speed.

And there, sitting on a rock at the very heart of the source, was the river boy.

He wore, as usual, nothing but the same black shorts, despite the cool of the early morning, and didn't seem at all surprised to see her. He said nothing but simply nodded, somewhat gravely, to her.

She stood before him, feeling slightly awkward, and waiting for him to speak. But he seemed lost in thought and certainly in no way grateful to her for dragging herself up here in the early hours of the morning to help him with a thing he hadn't even told her about.

She was just starting to feel a little nettled about this when he smiled at her.

'Thank you for coming,' he said.

She felt herself blush but he merely smiled again, then nodded past her.

'Look.'

She turned and gazed back down the slope in the direction of the fall, and there, below her, clear in the morning light, she saw the valley rolling away to the west and the river weaving a path through it towards the sea.

And, far away in the distance, to her astonishment and joy, was the sea itself, floating, it seemed, like a deep blue cloud.

She looked down at the stream. It was hard to believe that this tiny current was linked to that full-bodied ocean whose outer limits she saw in the distance.

She thought of Grandpa again, standing here as a boy, gazing at the sea in just the same way, lost in wonder, no doubt, as she was. What had he thought in those far-off days, as he stood here, alone with the sky and the wind? How had he seen all this, with his artist's eye?

She sat down beside the river boy, her eyes still on the ocean.

'I didn't know we could see that far.' She found she

was whispering, as though she were in some sacred place. 'It's like . . . it's like . . . '

'Like seeing a whole life,' he said.

'A whole life?' She looked round at him, though she already sensed what he meant.

'The life of the river.' His eyes remained fixed on the horizon. 'It's born here and it runs its allotted distance, sometimes fast, sometimes slow, sometimes straight, sometimes twisting, sometimes calm, sometimes turbulent, and it keeps on running until it reaches its end in the sea. I find that comforting.'

'In what way?'

'Just to know that whatever happens to the river on its journey, it'll end up in something beautiful.'

'But death isn't beautiful,' she said, thinking of Grandpa.

'It's dying that isn't beautiful,' he said, still gazing at the sea. 'But then, living isn't always beautiful either. This river will have its battles on the way but it'll keep on running because it has to. And even when it reaches the end, it'll already have started renewing itself here. I find that comforting, too.'

She wasn't sure what he was trying to tell her but she said nothing. He was silent for a while, then he spoke again.

'I'm leaving this place today.'

She looked at him.

'Leaving? But why?'

'It's time to let the river go.'

'Let it . . . go?'

He nodded.

'I've got to let it go now. I mustn't hang on to it. But there's one thing still to do.' He glanced at her. 'I'm going to swim down to the sea.'

She gave a start.

'Are you out of your mind? It's twenty-five miles away.'

'As the crow flies. Forty-three and a quarter miles if you follow the river.'

'Forty-three and—'

'It'll take several hours. But the current will do lots of the work. I know I can do it. I'll walk and wade from here until I can start swimming.'

She stared at him, unsure whether to be concerned or impressed. But his next words threw her mind into turmoil.

'Come with me.'

'What?'

'Come with me. Please. I'm a bit scared of going on my own.'

'But—'

'Please.' His eyes burned with that fire she had seen the first day they met. 'It'll be tough but you can do it. You were born to swim. Haven't you always wanted to do something like this?'

The vision danced inside her, madly enticing: a journey from source to sea—it was indeed the kind of challenge she had always craved as a swimmer. But she knew what her answer had to be.

'I can't leave Grandpa. You know I can't.'

The fire in his eyes seemed slowly to dim, and he looked away, back towards the sea; and she felt a sudden, almost overwhelming sadness as she realized how much this strange boy yearned for her to swim with him; and though she knew she could not join him, she sensed that she was failing him, and—in some strange way—herself, too.

He spoke again, his voice as faraway as the sea towards which his mind now seemed to travel.

'Your grandfather will be all right. You don't need to worry about him any more.'

She looked at him, wondering how he could speak with such certainty or whether he was just trying to be comforting. But he merely glanced towards her and nodded.

'I'll see you.'

And without another word he stood up and set off

down the slope towards the fall, walking only in the stream. She followed, a few steps behind, not in the stream but clumping over the uneven grass. Before long the head of the fall loomed before them and she stopped close to the edge, wondering what he would do next.

He stood there, motionless, at the very lip of the fall, the water streaming past his legs so fast she felt it must surely carry him away. But he was as still as a rock, gazing ahead towards his far-off destination. Then, without a word or glance towards her, he dived.

Her mouth dropped open and she stared; and, in that moment, she saw crystallized the perfect symmetry of the river boy as he moved through the air, a creature of beauty and grace, part fish, part bird, part human, part something else: something she could not define but which defined him—a part he had shared with her.

He plunged into the pool and surfaced a few feet beyond the throw of the torrent, his black hair streaming amid the bubbling eddies; then he turned and struck out across the pool towards the outlet, the current moving him swiftly down. He reached the shallow part of the pool, waded to the end where the stream rushed away down the slope, climbed over and strode off through the trees, the water washing round his feet.

A moment later he was gone.

She looked at the rush of water close by her as it slid over the fall like a shiny tongue, then scattered into flight; and she too felt the urge to dive, to throw herself from the top, and race and chase that foaming torrent.

It didn't look dangerous: this was only a smallish waterfall, not much higher than the top board at the pool back home, and she had dived off that often enough. There were no rocks directly underneath, the plunge pool was good and deep; and the river boy had just done it. She had her swimsuit on, as always, ready for action; all she had to do was throw her T-shirt and shoes down, walk to the lip, compose herself just as he had done, and dive.

But she knew she could not.

And she knew why not.

With a pang of shame, she drew back from the fall and started to climb down.

But that now presented serious problems. Coming up, it had been fairly easy to see the handholds and footholds, but this way was different. She tried to retrace the route she had taken on the way up but the rock now felt strange and hostile and, a short way down, she stopped.

She had lost her way already. She held on tight, the water roaring in her ears, and glanced down. Below her was the outer edge of the pool, a few feet to the side of the plunging water. She was too far to the left; she had climbed up closer to the torrent.

She glanced to the right at the water thundering past her and the glistening rockface. The descent seemed much too dangerous here, yet she had climbed up this way, so it had to be possible.

She hesitated, then stretched towards the fall, searching for one of the handholds she had used earlier. To her relief, she felt a jutting rock too jagged to be slippery. She hadn't seen it on the way up but she was grateful for it now. She edged to the right, holding on to it with both hands while she swung her foot about, struggling to find something to stand on.

After a moment she felt a crevice in the rock and tested her weight against it. It held and she eased herself down a few inches, stretching her other foot out for something else to support her. For a few harrowing seconds she felt nothing but the shiny surface of rock against her foot, then at last she found a tiny crack, almost too small but mercifully wide enough to dig her toe into and lower herself a little further.

She breathed hard and looked down.

She would have to let go of the jagged rock now and find something further down to cling to. She scrabbled about with one hand and found another crack, then thrust out her foot which brushed against a small fissure.

She tested its strength and lowered herself down. Below her, to one side, she saw another fissure and quickly pushed her other foot into that, twisting her face away from the spray which now burst over her from the base of the fall.

To her relief, the rockface below her was covered with cracks. She eased herself to the left, away from the plunge pool, and, a few moments later, she was down.

She looked up at the fall, still feeling somewhat ashamed. It was no use telling herself that Mum and Dad wouldn't have wanted her to dive, and that probably even Grandpa would have advised her against it.

The river boy had dived.

And she could have done so, too.

She ran down the slope, now anxious about the time. She had taken much longer reaching the source than she'd expected, and had not meant to linger there, and then there was the difficulty climbing the rockface.

As she ran, she thought of the river boy and his dream, and what he had asked her to do; and she found herself running faster and faster, desperate to catch him up.

Just to say goodbye.

But she did not see him. He had gone on ahead, even though he was frightened. And she had never found out who he was after all.

The sun rose higher; the air grew warmer. She raced on, down the slope and into the valley, and finally stumbled into the clearing by the cottage.

To her surprise, the car was gone.

And Alfred was standing there.

Chapter Seventeen

Something was wrong; something was dreadfully wrong. She could tell from his face; and there was a strange silence everywhere. Even the river seemed muted.

'What's happened?' she demanded.

Alfred had no gift for brevity but he did his best.

'It's your old grandpa. He's had another attack, a serious one, and your mum and dad have taken him to the hospital at Braymouth. They couldn't wait for you to get back. There wasn't any time. It was all too quick. They got him in the car somehow and stopped by my cottage, and your mum rushed to the door to tell me what's what and to ask me to come down here and look after you, and then she was back in the car again and they were off and—'

'But Grandpa, is he—?'

'He's still alive.' Alfred's tone was as measured and unhurried as if he were talking about the weather but his face betrayed his concern. 'But I won't lie to you,' he said. 'He looked terrible even from where I was standing and I could see he was in a lot of pain.'

She glanced frantically towards the lane.

'I've got to be with him. I've got to get to Braymouth. I've—'

But Alfred shook his head.

'Your mum said to wait here with me.'

'But Grandpa!' She stared at him in desperation. 'I've got to be with him. Can't you see?'

He put a hand on her shoulder.

'I understand how you feel. Really I do. But your mum reckons it's best you don't see him like he is. He looked so bad, it would really upset you, and it would upset him, too, I'm sure, to have you see him like that. You know what a proud old man he is. Your mum did say she thought it was maybe as well you weren't there when it happened.'

She turned away, unable to look at him.

'But he needs me,' she murmured. 'He can't die without me there.'

'You must be brave, Jessica. Look, your mum gave me the mobile phone and said they'll ring just as soon as there's any news.'

'We could phone them,' said Jess eagerly.

But he shook his head.

'They won't be there yet. Not for a while. You can't go fast on the Braymouth Road, especially with a sick man in the car. No, you'll have to be patient.'

Jess turned away. Her mind was filled with pain, and it was the pain of failure. She had failed Grandpa by not being there at the very moment he needed her most.

She didn't blame Mum and Dad for wanting to shield her from this. They were only trying to be sensitive to her and Grandpa. But the thought that she could not see Grandpa at all now filled her with distress.

Alfred nodded towards the door.

'Come inside and have something to eat. It might do you some good.'

'I'm not hungry.'

'Well, let's go in anyway. I'm a bit weary on my legs. I'm not used to moving about so fast.'

She followed him, too stunned to think of anything but Grandpa. On the kitchen table was a plate of crusty rolls and a jar of honey.

'My daughter made those rolls,' he said proudly. 'She's a dab hand at bread making. Go on, I promised your mum I'd make sure you had something to eat and you don't want me to get into trouble, do you? And anyway, you don't know when you'll get another chance to eat today.'

She still didn't want to eat; she couldn't think of eating.

'Go on,' he urged her. 'Do it for me.'

She sat down—anything to stop him fussing—and ate the rolls in silence, her mind locked on Grandpa and, to her surprise, an image of the river boy, driving his body stroke by stroke towards the sea. She did not know why that picture came to her so strongly when all she wanted to think of was Grandpa, but it grew in her mind, powerful and clear until it almost dominated the dark vision of the old man's face.

She finished the rolls, then wandered out to the stream and sat beside it, wondering about Grandpa and whether he was still alive. It was possible he had not even made it to the hospital. Yet something told her he was still alive; and that he was thinking of her right this moment.

To her relief, Alfred left her alone with her thoughts. But then, about twenty minutes later, he came out and wandered over to join her.

'I meant to ask you,' he said. 'What do you think of the portrait?'

She looked up at him.

'What portrait?'

'Your grandpa's. The self-portrait.'

She frowned.

'I didn't know he'd done a self-portrait. Where is it?'

'In the sitting room. I was looking at it before you got here.'

She hurried in to the sitting room but all she saw was Grandpa's river picture propped against the wall. Alfred lumbered up behind her.

'Funny old picture,' he said. 'He's captured it, though.'

She looked round at him.

'What are you talking about? That's a river scene.'

Alfred studied the picture for a moment, then burst out laughing.

'Well, I'm blowed, you're right! There is a river in it. Never saw that. Well, it figures. He always had a thing about the river.'

'What do you mean?'

'Well, he was obsessed with it. Used to spend all his time swimming. He was good, too. Could have been a champion distance swimmer if he'd trained properly but he never had the discipline. He used to go on about how he was going to swim the length of the river one day, all the way from source to sea. Well, I never saw him do it. Still, he left the area when he was your age, just after his parents died, so I guess he didn't have the chance. I don't suppose he'll do it now.'

His words entered her like bullets. She stared back at the picture and suddenly saw it as if for the first time. The dappled black for the hair, the misty trails in the water for the nose and mouth, the dark spots that could be eyes—there *was* a face here, a face she could not believe she had missed, a face she had seen only a short while ago gazing from the top of the fall.

There was no time to lose.

She ran into the hall, kicked off her shoes and tore the T-shirt off from on top of her swimsuit. Alfred called through from the sitting room.

'Everything all right, Jessica?'

But she didn't answer. Without a backward glance she rushed out of the cottage, down to the bank where Grandpa had finished his painting, and threw herself into the water.

And the river opened and took her into itself.

Chapter Eighteen

The first three hours she barely noticed. The time she knew only from the rhythm of her stroke, a rhythm so practised and so regular it was like watching the breathing of a sleeping child. And her body, a healthy, well-trained creature with an existence seemingly apart from her, did her bidding and left her to her thoughts.

But her thoughts were painful things. They took her to a hospital bed in Braymouth; they took her to an unseen swimmer somewhere ahead of her, a swimmer so strong and so accomplished she knew she was unlikely to catch him, unless he stopped.

But he would not stop; surely he would not stop. What had he to stop for now? She had let him go on, thinking she did not care.

In the futility of that thought, she plunged on in the chase, dimly taking in the changing form of the river as she drove herself down its slippery body, pushed on by the current and by the tide of her will.

Banks slipped by, and rocks, and eddies that pushed and pulled at her but didn't hold her back. She glided down the river like a sprite, pursuing the boy she could not see yet sensed ahead of her, pulling her on, just as the sea pulled him.

And with every stroke, the images of Grandpa kept falling over her like spray.

Two more hours passed, three, four; but she was losing track of time. The more she swam, the more time ceased to matter. All that mattered was now, here, breathing in, breathing out, head down in this weird, watery world.

She swam on, fighting the tiredness that was starting to seep through her body. The ecstasy of co-ordination she usually felt in her strokes was gone now. She knew she had never swum like this before but there was still no sign of the river boy, and there was a long way to go before she reached Braymouth.

If she reached Braymouth.

She didn't know how fast the current was moving her. It could take many more hours yet, perhaps more hours than she had the strength for. But she must not stop. She must keep going. She must try and catch the river boy, even though she was frightened at the thought of what he was.

Yet she knew there was no need for fear. There was no evil in all this, only magic. The river boy was not a curse but a benediction; a blessing in the history of Grandpa's life, and in her own small existence. And here she was, swimming after all, and with a challenge to match her greatest hopes.

She wondered what Alfred had done. Probably looked for her when she didn't come back and then rung the hospital; so no doubt Mum and Dad were worrying about her now, and maybe even Grandpa.

She felt a rush of guilt but there was nothing to be done. She couldn't stop; she wouldn't stop. She would swim on and on, for ever if need be, until she saw the river boy one last time.

And the river ran with her, like a dream wandering through a sleeping mind.

Despair, when it came, crept up on her slowly, like a dark predator fish that follows in secret, biding its time, knowing it will conquer in the end. She swam on, somehow, fighting this new sick feeling inside her.

She knew it was not a sickness of her body, which still fumbled on through its strokes, weary though they were; it was a sickness of the will, born of knowledge that after all this time and effort, without even a glimpse of the river boy, she would never catch him now; that even if she made it to Braymouth, Grandpa would be gone and his spirit swum away for ever, and all she would have left was this empty trail.

Despair bit into her and she saw Grandpa's face in the darkness of her mind, the face she had always loved and smiled at, even when he didn't smile at her. And she tried to hold on to that face, picture it, cling to it, as though it might give her strength; and, in a strange way, it did.

But she was so weary now and her thoughts were of defeat. This was the point, she knew, that Channel swimmers sometimes reach, the hurdle she'd read about that they have to overcome when doubts and fears crowd in and urge them to stop and climb back into the boat, and go home.

But there was no boat here, only the verdant banks and sloping fields of an unknown land she glimpsed as she glanced up to snatch her tiny pocket of air.

There was no stopping now, no swimming to the bank for a rest or to walk. Where would she walk? Only the river could take her to him.

She threw her mind back to the swimming and tried to push herself on, tried to tell herself she had something in reserve. Every part of her seemed to ache now, every part of her seemed to beg her to stop: her arms, her legs, her shoulders; her thoughts.

She wanted to cry so much. She wanted to cry about Grandpa, about herself, about the figure ahead of her, somewhere out of sight; the figure in whose wake she followed, in whose wake she had always followed.

She had thought she might just catch him. But she was tired now, so tired, and living off the scraps of her spirit.

She stopped and trod water, and tried to collect herself. At least coldness had not struck, too. The sun was a long way past its zenith and the water was well warmed.

She looked about her. The banks were still densely wooded but the valley sides had receded with the miles and fields now climbed away on either side, broken by hedgerows and stone walls. The river itself was widening all the time. She gasped suddenly.

Far ahead down the river, almost out of view.

A swimmer.

She watched, struggling with her feelings, trying to see more. It had to be him. It could be no one else.

She struck out again with as much energy as her exhausted body would allow. She knew this would be her only chance, and, if she didn't catch the river boy this time, with what little strength she had left, she would lose him for ever. She drove herself on, trying, when she could, to keep him in view.

Yet every time she looked, he seemed just as far ahead, just as far out of reach. She swam on, trying to break the distance between them but still it refused to lessen.

What seemed like another hour passed; or perhaps it was only ten minutes. She no longer knew nor cared. She gauged time only by the depth of pain. She forced her attention from herself to the figure ahead, trying to ignore the growing feeling that he was an illusion, a trick of the mind, a creation of her longing.

She stopped suddenly, and lifted her face from the water, and tried to see the figure again.

And this time there was no sign.

It was gone; for ever, surely. It had been no more than an illusion after all, a product of her insecurity. She breathed hard and swam on, knowing nothing else to do now.

And the strokes went on, mechanically, almost by themselves, it seemed, driven by no will of hers any more but by the body's remnant power; a power that was waning fast.

An hour later, or two hours, or three, or however long it was, she looked up again from the belly of the river and saw the sun falling over the horizon ahead. She stopped and stared dumbly about her, having noticed or remembered little of her surroundings for some time.

To her surprise, she found herself in the middle of a small estuary. Just ahead were boats on moorings and she could see flat, grassy land on either side, and a rugby pitch, and the remains of an old fort, and further down, a sea wall and slipways, and buildings.

And, for the first time, waves pushing in from the sea.

Braymouth. She had made it to Braymouth after all.

But she had lost everything.

She tried to swim again, breast-stroke now, pushing the water back with tired, aimless strokes. But this time her body did not respond.

She had nothing left. Just enough strength, perhaps, to struggle to the bank and stumble the rest of the way. There was no point in staying in the water now. She had tried and failed. She turned to the right and faced the bank, and tried to steel her body to swim towards it.

But instead she found herself sobbing, sobbing as she had done that day the river boy first spoke to her. All was lost: Grandpa was surely dead and his spirit had swum away without her into the sea. And only her tears were flowing after him.

The voice, when it came, was like the first time she had ever heard it: quiet and tender and concerned. Even the words were the same.

'Why are you crying?'

She started and turned, and looked into the eyes of the river boy.

He was just a few feet from her, treading water as she was, but without any trace of the pain or exhaustion she felt. Indeed, he looked as though he had just dived in from the other bank and swum up behind her, full of energy; and there was an elation in his eyes, a sense of joy.

He swam closer, watching her all the time, and stopped within arm's length; and spoke again, softly.

'Did you think I wouldn't wait for you?'

She was crying still, crying into the waves that washed over her as they slanted in from the sea, but she tried to speak, tried to tell him something of what she felt.

But he smiled and shook his head.

'Don't speak,' he said quietly. 'You don't need to. Just swim with me a little longer.'

And he turned to the side and began to swim on towards the sea.

She followed, weary still yet strengthened by the wonder of his presence. He did not swim fast, just a slow, even crawl, his head down and not looking her way; and she swam with him, filled with awe and deep, churning emotion.

And, as they drew closer to the mouth of the estuary, her feeling of wonder deepened. The river had changed so much during its journey, and here, close to its end, she knew she was on the cusp of something deep and powerful and infinitely mysterious.

She looked across at the river boy, still swimming quietly beside her. There was no mystery in him now, and nothing to be frightened of after all.

She felt more tears start and dug her face under the water again so that he wouldn't see them. Exhaustion was starting to master her again and she knew she would have to head for the shore soon or she might not have the strength to reach safety.

But the river boy—she couldn't leave the river boy, not now that she had finally found him again. She lifted her head from the water and looked to the side.

And, to her dismay, saw that he was gone.

She stared in desperation at the space where he had been. But she saw only sea now. And she suddenly realized that, just as the boy was gone, so too was the river.

They had indeed reached the sea.

Close by was the extremity of the sea wall and, behind it, kiosks, shops, amusement arcades, a café, a chip shop; and houses. It seemed inconceivable that she could have swum past without noticing all this, or being noticed herself.

But so little was inconceivable now.

She gazed back out to sea and understood at last; then struck out for the shore, praying the tide would not sweep her out.

But the sea was kind to her and her final, flagging strokes felt almost relaxing. She saw a slipway, made for it, and hauled herself out of the water, shivering and spent.

Far out to sea the sun was close to the horizon. The day was almost done and she knew her journey was over.

Just as Grandpa's was, too.

Chapter Nineteen

It was there, curled up on the slipway, that the policewoman found her.

'Are you all right, love?'

Jess turned with an effort and saw the woman standing over her. At the edge of the road, close to the top of the slipway, was a police car, and a tall policeman standing beside it. Nearby, a small knot of onlookers observed proceedings.

The policewoman spoke again.

'Would you, by any chance, be Jessica?'

Jess frowned as the full import of the trouble and pain she must have caused Mum and Dad rushed upon her.

'Yes,' she said quickly. 'Listen, I've got to get to the hospital. It's urgent.'

The policewoman seemed reassuringly understanding.

'No problem. Come on, let's get you away from all the prying eyes.'

She helped Jess to her feet and up the slipway to the car. The policeman put a jacket round her and she sat in the back with the woman, and they drove off through the little town.

'Here,' said the woman, passing her a sandwich. 'Peanut butter. Hope you like it. It's all I've got.'

'It's all she's ever got,' said the policeman from the front. 'She'd put peanut butter in her coffee if she could.'

The policewoman laughed.

'Never mind him,' she said to Jess. 'He's got no taste. You go ahead and eat.'

'Thank you.' She hated peanut butter but she ate the sandwich gratefully. 'What time is it?' she said dully.

'Nine o'clock,' said the policewoman.

Nine o'clock.

She'd been in the water about eleven hours. People had swum the Channel in that time. She stared out of the window, unsure what to feel.

The policeman was passing on a message to the hospital.

'She's fine,' he was saying, 'just tired and cold . . . been in the sea . . . right, yep, we'll bring her straight there . . . '

She thought of Mum and Dad receiving the news and wondered what they were thinking; and what they would say.

'How did you find me?' she said.

The policewoman answered.

'Your mum rang us at about two o'clock from the hospital. She'd had a call from the old fellow living near your cottage some time before to say you'd gone missing. He said you'd left the house and gone off somewhere and when you didn't come back, he got worried. Your mum left it a bit, then when you still didn't turn up, she called us and we went out to look. Spent most of the afternoon searching the river and the countryside round the cottage. But your mum kept telling us—'

'My mum was with you?' Jess stared at her, horrified at the thought of Mum leaving Grandpa on her account.

The policeman spoke.

'Your mum wasn't with us. We kept in touch by phone. There didn't seem much point in either of your parents joining the search round the cottage, especially with your Grandpa so ill. We had plenty of our people there, and those folk from the other cottage helped, too.' He shook his head. 'But we should have listened to your mum and started the search from this end. Could have saved us hours.'

126

Jess looked at him.

'What did my mum say?'

He shook his head.

'Quite a woman, your mum. Unflappable, you know what I mean? She said you weren't the kind of girl to do anything stupid and that you were too good a swimmer to drown, unless something really unlucky happened, and that you often swam for three or four hours at a stretch, so probably you were upset about your grandpa and wanted to swim your anxieties off. Then, when you hadn't turned up by two o'clock, she started to get a bit more worried and said you might just have got it into your head to swim all the way to Braymouth.'

He chuckled.

'Well, none of us gave that idea a moment's thought and neither did the old boy at the cottage, so we went on hunting round the river and in the woods. Should have listened to your mum all along.'

She stared out of the window, thinking of the strange events of this day, a day which still had not run its course. But the last part was before her now.

They had reached the hospital.

Mum was waiting outside the entrance. Jess ran to her and threw her arms round her.

'Mum, I'm so sorry . . . I didn't mean . . . I didn't mean . . . '

'Sssh,' said Mum, stroking her hair. 'It's all right. It's all right. Tell me about it later. I know you've done something very brave. But now I want you to be even braver.'

Jess looked up at her, her eyes dim with tears.

'It's all right, Mum. I know he's gone. And I know he's OK.'

Mum looked down at her, still stroking her hair, then glanced at the policewoman beside them.

'Thank you for all you've done. I'm sorry we've caused you so much trouble. Whose jacket is this?'

'My colleague's. The gentleman in the car.'

Mum looked round at him.

'You must have this back,' she called. 'We can find something for Jess inside.'

He wound down the window.

'You hang on to it for a bit,' he said. 'We'll be sticking around for a while, just to tie up loose ends.' He caught Jess's eye and grinned. 'Looks nicer on you than it does on me anyway.'

Mum smiled at him, then turned to the policewoman.

'Can we talk in a few minutes? I want to take my daughter to see her grandfather.'

'Of course.'

Mum put an arm round Jess's shoulder.

'Come on, love.'

They walked into the hospital, ignoring the quizzical glance of the receptionist at the barefoot girl clad only in a swimsuit and ill-fitting jacket, and made their way down the corridor towards a room at the end.

So this was the place: a tiny place for the end of a huge life; or at least a life of huge achievement. Not that Grandpa would have seen it that way; no doubt he had been thinking right to the end of all the things he hadn't had time to do.

She entered the room and saw him lying on the bed, and her father standing over him. Dad turned and saw her, and hurried forward, and threw his arms around her; she reached out and held him.

'Dad, I'm sorry, I'm—'

'It's all right. It's all right. Just as long as you're safe. That's all that matters.'

They finally drew apart and, together with Mum, turned to face the bed.

'He died half an hour ago,' said Mum.

She looked down at the face of this beautiful, strange old man, and there was no pain there, no anger, no disappointment; it was so perfectly still it seemed almost like a painting, a painting he himself might have done. She had never seen him like this.

But then, this was not Grandpa any more. The Grandpa she had seen and would always know was a different Grandpa, a Grandpa who was ever alive, ever youthful, ever strong.

'He was amazing at the end,' said Mum. 'I wouldn't have believed it. He seemed to feel no distress at all. And he kept talking about you.'

Jess looked at her.

'Me?'

Mum nodded.

'During the day, when the police were looking for you, he wouldn't stop talking about you. The strange thing is, we didn't tell him you were missing or anything because we didn't want to distress him in his last moments. But he seemed to understand something was wrong and he kept on saying: "Don't worry about Jess. Don't worry about Jess. She's going to be OK. She's going to be OK." He was very emphatic about it. We found it really comforting.'

Jess looked away towards the window. Someone had placed flowers there and the last rays of the sun were catching them. She thought of Grandpa, and what he had said.

Yes, she was going to be OK. She wasn't OK yet; she wouldn't be OK for some time; but she would be OK one day. She would grieve, just like Mum and Dad, especially Dad, and her grief would be deep, and it would hurt her.

But she wanted that grief: she knew it was natural and right, just as the passing of this strange and wonderful old man was natural and right, just as her own death would one day be natural and right. But there was much living to do first, much living, much growing.

Much swimming.

In the wake of the river boy.

Dad had sat down again by Grandpa's side and was gazing at his face. Mum caught Jess's eye and drew her back a few feet.

'There's another strange thing that happened,' she whispered. 'Something to do with your father.'

She eyed Dad for a moment but he was still staring at Grandpa's face, lost in thought.

'Just before he died,' she said, 'he asked Dad to lean closer to him so he could speak. I don't know what he said—it didn't last more than a few moments—but since then your dad's hardly stopped crying. And I don't mean out of pain. He hasn't told me what Pop said, but I'll tell you one thing, there were no differences between them at the end.'

Jess turned away and stared once more at the flowers by the window. And she remembered what she had yearned for yet been unable to speak of, that time Grandpa had asked what he could do for her. She had not expected this; but Grandpa, as always, had surprised her.

She heard sounds in the corridor, footsteps and voices, all discreetly low. Thoughts of the world and the business of living started to filter back, and with them came the exhaustion she had somehow fought off or forgotten, here in the presence of death.

There would be the police to speak to, and the hospital staff, and Mum would want her to have a medical check-up after her marathon swim, and there would be arrangements to be made about Grandpa's body, and . . .

She turned to the door. People were coming in now, a doctor and two nurses, then the policewoman and the policeman, and another nurse, all grave and respectful. She felt a moment of annoyance at their intrusion; but Mum smiled at them and put her arm round her again, and they all stood there in silence and looked down on the calm, still face of Grandpa.

Chapter Twenty

She never said anything about the river boy. When they asked her what happened, she simply said that she had swum; that she had needed to swim and had not meant to worry them all.

The story of the river boy remained locked within her. Somehow she felt he was a secret she was meant to keep to herself, a secret more precious to her than ever now that he was gone.

Yet during the next few days, while Mum and Dad busied with the funeral arrangements, she still found, as she wandered by the river, that she was looking for him.

It didn't matter that she knew he was gone. Indeed, she would not have wanted to see him again now; the spirit of Grandpa had set off on a new adventure and she would not want to hold him back. He had left her the painting, Dad said, and she could see him whenever she wanted.

The ceremony at the Braymouth crematorium was simple, just as Grandpa would have liked it. They had considered having his body taken home for the funeral but quickly discounted the idea: this was the place he had wanted to return to—the only part of his past he had ever acknowledged. It was only right that he should be put to rest here.

Alfred was with them, looking distinctly awkward in a suit and tie, and Mr and Mrs Gray; and that was all. The service was brief and afterwards they wandered out to the gardens overlooking the sea. Dad was crying again but Jess no longer worried about him as she had done.

He would be well now, just as she, too, would be well—in time, when the worst of the pain was gone. And he had Mum, as strong and unflinching as ever, and herself, ready to give him everything she could; and they each had their memories.

The following afternoon he drove back to Braymouth on his own and returned with Grandpa's ashes in a small metal urn.

'I've been trying to think on the way back what to do with these,' he said, putting the urn on the table.

Jess looked at it and felt something stir inside her, a strange inner certainty she would have to express. But Mum spoke first.

'What would Pop have wanted done with them?'

Dad shrugged.

'Don't suppose he ever gave it a thought. You know he was as uninterested in the future as he was in the past. Think of the trouble we had getting him to make a will.'

'But what would he tell us to do with them if we could ask him now?'

'Chuck 'em in the bin probably, urn and all.'

'We can't do that.'

'No, obviously. I suppose we could take them home and scatter them in the garden, or bury the urn completely and plant a tree, or—'

'Dad.' Jess had to speak now.

Mum and Dad both looked across at her.

'Dad, I . . . I know what Grandpa would have wanted.'

There was a silence; a silence in which she almost felt she caught the listening presence of Grandpa himself.

Dad watched her for a moment, his eyes searching her face.

'Do you want to take them?' he said.

She felt herself colour.

'Not on my own. It wouldn't be right. I mean, we should all be together for this. I shouldn't . . . have them to myself.'

'But is that what you want?' His voice was very low, but, to her relief, without resentment.

She nodded; and he smiled at last.

'Then take them, my love.'

Early next morning, the day they were to leave, she put on her swimsuit, placed the urn inside her duffle bag, slung the bag on her back and left the cottage, heading up the slope.

It was a bright, clear day and the sound of the river seemed louder, livelier, more irrepressible than ever. She stepped off the path and into the water and strode up against the current, the rocks hard and lumpy under her bare feet but tolerable enough as she made her way up the cool, splashing stream. And, as she walked, she tried to drink in all that she saw and heard and felt.

Because she knew she would never come back to this place. To return would be to destroy a spell, a spell that had fallen upon her for a few short days but now was passing from her life. Better to leave this place sacred, just as she had found it, and let the enchantment live on in memory.

But the spell was not yet over.

There was still this last thing to do, and then she could go home and recommence her life. She wandered on, staying in the stream, just as the river boy had done on his way down, and she did not stop until she had reached the upland lake where she had first seen him, standing at the top of the fall.

She looked up at it, plunging down with ebullient power, as timeless and majestic as ever; then, without hesitation, began to climb.

This time the ascent was easy, even without her shoes on. She felt somehow as light as gossamer, as though her body were nothing more than a thought, a whisper, as ephemeral as a cloud; her hand reached straight to holds they seemed to know in advance, holds different to the ones she had used the last time.

She reached the top, took the urn from her bag and studied it for a moment as the light caught it; then she threw the empty bag down onto the rocks at the base of the fall and walked on up the rise, and did not stop until she had reached the source— the place where she had sat with the boy and seen the river's life. And she sat down again on that same small rock and gazed out again.

And there in the distance, unchanged yet ever-changing, was the sea.

She bent down and looked at the mushy ground, at the water oozing up from it as if by some mysterious power, then took the lid off the urn and stared at the strange powdery ash.

And her thoughts ran back to Grandpa again, and she remembered his face as she had always known it, with its wicked eyes and laughing mouth, and she thought of his cussedness, his cantankerousness, his sense of humour and . . .

And all that he had been.

And somehow still was.

And she looked at the ashes and shook her head. These ashes were not Grandpa. They were soft and unresistant, moving according to her will as she tipped the urn from side to side; so unlike him.

The real Grandpa was not here. The real Grandpa was as free as wind and water and sky. He was feeling no pain over this and neither would she.

She tipped the urn and let a tiny portion of the ashes trickle into the water from the source. The water collected them and they started to run down with the current, some catching against the soft earth at the sides but most of them floating down like tiny seeds towards the greater stream.

She thought back to what the boy had said about the river; that even when it reaches the end, it'll already have started renewing itself here. She hadn't understood him then; but she understood now.

She tipped again and sprinkled more ashes into the water, and watched them float away, specks of Grandpa's life but no longer part of him, nothing to cling on to, nothing to hold him back.

Or her.

Life would go on again. There was no need for pain, only a wholesome sorrow which would, in time, relent. She looked into the urn and saw it was half-full, and stood up and started to walk down in the stream, sprinkling little trails into the water ahead of her and following them down towards the head of the fall.

And when she reached the lip and stood there, just as the river boy had done only a short time before, and felt the power of the stream breaking over her legs and thrusting down into its mad descent, she knew that the spirit of Grandpa was not here in this place of magic, but in her, in Mum and Dad, in Alfred, in everyone who had ever known him.

But the spirit of the river boy was in her alone.

She raised her arm and tipped the urn one final time; and the last of the ashes scattered into flight, to be lost in bubbling life. She stared after them, tears starting again, then threw the urn down into the water.

And dived after it.

And, as she flew down, the air ruffling her face, she caught the river boy's presence one last time.

Other Books by Tim Bowler

Shadows
ISBN 0 19 271802 9

Jamie's father keeps driving him on to win, to become a world squash champion. But Jamie can't take it any more and is desperate to get away.

Then he finds a girl hiding in his shed, and in helping her to escape from the danger that is pursuing her, he is at last able to deal with his own problems.

He realizes he can't run away for ever. He has to come out of the shadows and face up to his father, whatever the cost.

Dragon's Rock
ISBN 0 19 275036 4

Benjamin knows he shouldn't have taken the stone from Dragon's Rock. Ever since then, he's had the same terrifying nightmare of the dragon that chases him, breath like a furnace, roaring in fury, racing faster, faster . . .

Midget
ISBN 0 19 275037 2

Midget doesn't have much going for him. He's fifteen years old, three foot tall, and puny as anything. He's trapped in a useless, twitching body he can't control, tortured by Seb, his cruel older brother, and can only communicate in grunts and gestures.

But Midget knows one thing—sailing. He dreams of sailing his own boat, and showing Seb a thing or two. Everyone says it'll take a miracle, but that's when Midget starts to realize that even miracles are possible. It's just that sometimes they hurt people who get in the way . . .

'a masterly handling of suspense and cold trickling horror'
Sunday Telegraph